Bossy Grump Next Door

Ava Nichols

Chapter 1

Rose

I'm starting to worry that maybe my family is right when they tell me I'm unlucky.

Most people would probably jump at the chance to house-sit the gorgeous mansion that my cousin calls home, but for me, it's not really a privilege. It's a necessity. Chloe's letting me live here while she's off in Europe with her latest beau because I have nowhere else to go. My landlord kicked me out when I couldn't pay rent after several months of late payments, and I can't afford to move back across the country to my parents' place.

I wouldn't do it anyway. That would lead to failure.

I know my family's just waiting for me to give up, leave Los Angeles, pack it in, and admit defeat, but I refuse. I didn't go to the fashion institute and get my degree and saddle myself with all this student debt just so I could slink back home and get a job working as a secretary in Dad's local packing company,

No. I'm going to make it. I might not be someone in the film industry, hoping to become a star but I fit right in with all the other dreamers who have moved here from some-where else, somewhere far less interesting and far too small.

I won't give in.

I use the last of my money to pack my meager belong-ings into a cheap storage unit, then drive over to Chloe's place in Bel Air. The moment I cross over into the neighbor-hood, I can feel the change. I'm on edge, knowing I can't really afford to even breathe in this area.

The houses are huge, and the streets are quiet and lined with massive trees. Shrubbery and strategic plants keep a lot of the houses partially obscured from view, providing privacy. The streets are wide, well-maintained, and I feel like if I yelled I'd be breaking some kind of rule.

I follow the instructions on my phone's GPS app until I turn onto the driveway in front of a large, glistening white house. It's not really my style —too many pillars. It makes me feel like I'm about to walk into a museum about the American Revolution rather than entering a home. But, it's Chloe's house, so as long as she likes it, I suppose. I'm just house-sitting for a few months while I save up some money.

Chloe bursts out of the house the moment I park the car. "You're here! You're here!"

She rushes up to me and pulls me into a hug that crushes me. That's Chloe for you, overenthusiastic about everything. "I'm so glad you came! Thank you so much, seriously."

"Of course, I'm glad I could help out."

"Well, we're helping each other, aren't we?" Chloe flings her arm around my shoulders and starts to lead me up the brick walkway to the house. "Sorry you're down on your luck again, Rose, you can't seem to shake it, huh?"

I grit my teeth and breathe slowly. "Yeah, that's just how it is sometimes."

She nods. "Well. Devon and I are so excited about this trip, and I'm so glad that you could housesit for us. I know we're doing you a favor but really, being able to have someone we really *trust* in the place..."

Devon, right, that's the name of her latest guy; thank God she brought him up because I wouldn't have been able to remember it for the life of me. She always has some new guy with her, and I can't ever keep track of them.

Unlike me. I can't remember the last time I had sex, never mind a romance. Then I look at Chloe's constant train of drama and heartbreak, and I wonder if any of it's worth it.

Chloe shows me around the house, explaining things like the laundry and the thermostat systems, the alarm system, when the gardeners come, and how to pay them. It feels like a job in and of itself just running this house. I honestly wonder how much it's worth it to live in a place like this when it requires this much attention.

"Oh, and if the HOA gives you any trouble, just pretend you're me." Chloe holds out her phone to show me her screen. "This is the NextDoor app; we use it to chat with our neighbors. If someone loses a dog or something, that's where you go. We look alike so I don't think anyone will notice you're not really me if they see you in person."

"Chloe, am I not supposed to be here?"

"No, no, it's fine. I just don't want any, y'know, drama or trouble."

I really don't want to know what drama or trouble Chloe thinks will happen if people realize that I'm her housesitting cousin, but I guess she has a point about us looking alike. We both have dark blonde hair and pale blue eyes, but I'm taller than Chloe, and less curvy.

I suppose if you don't really know Chloe all that well or

haven't seen her much, you could be fooled. I just hope I don't make some faux pas that comes back on the both of us.

"Well, I plan on just minding my own business," I promise. "I'm applying to jobs and I hope to hear back from one soon."

"What kind?"

"Admin stuff. Assistant work."

"The kind of stuff you'd be doing for your dad?"

I hide my wince. I can hear the undertone—*if you're just going to do that, why not do it at home instead of in expensive Los Angeles?*

"Yup. Just until I can get my fashion line off the ground."

"Of course, babe," Chloe says in that placating tone that my whole family uses whenever I bring up my plans.

I swallow my snippy words. I can't afford to piss Chloe off. If she changes her mind about letting me stay here, then I'm out on the street. I don't think she'd really do that, but it would be inconsiderate to try her patience. "What else do I need to know?"

Chloe finishes giving me the tour and explaining everything; then her phone goes off. "Oh! That's Devon. I'm meeting him for lunch at Yamashiro in Hollywood for an early dinner. Make yourself at home! We'll be heading out tomorrow."

Then she's gone in a flurry of motion and air kisses, and I'm alone in this massive house.

This place is so large that I feel like I'm going to get lost in it. It has seven bedrooms, a three-car garage, a swimming pool *and* a fountain in the backyard... and the living room ceiling is two stories high. It's insane.

I put my things in one of the side bedrooms and head

down to the home office to get to work on applications. This room looks like Chloe's never touched it, which doesn't surprise me. She inherited her money from her dad, my mom's brother, so she's never had to use an office a day in her life, home or otherwise.

There are a few promising jobs, but the one I apply for —that I really hope for—is as an executive assistant to the CEO for a hotel and resort company. I know that it might be a long shot, but I really do have over a decade of experience as an executive assistant. I started working for Dad's company when I was fourteen to earn pocket money, and I was practically running the place when I quit to get my degree in clothing design.

I don't think Dad's ever really forgiven me for that.

This job pays insanely well, though, and while it's probably because I'll be babysitting some spoiled brat of a CEO who makes decisions based on a whim and doesn't actually really do anything meaningful to run the company... but you know what? I can make it work, at least for a few months, while I get the finances to open up my store.

I know my designs are good. I just have to get started.

To my shock, the next day after I help Chloe get out the door, I find I have an email in reply to my application. I've been accepted, and they want me to come in for an interview.

Holy shit. I thought this was a long shot, but if it's actually possible... that would be amazing.

I try to go to bed early, pick out my most professional outfit, and set up my hair and makeup supplies on the vanity in Chloe's massive master bedroom beforehand. I want to look my absolute best. I even take some melatonin before bed so I'll be truly well-rested. And that's when I'm woken up at *five in the goddamn morning* by the sound of construction.

What the fuck!?

Chapter 2

Simon

I know that Mom thinks I'm crazy for doing this, but the fact is, if I don't actually do something with my hands, something productive, I'm going to go crazy and tank the company while I'm at it.

It wasn't my idea to take over the company in the first place. It was Dad's idea, and I agreed, vaguely, because he was hale and hearty and I figured I'd eventually find a way to change his mind. There were plenty of hungry young men who worked with my Dad. I was sure he'd take one of them under his wing and he'd have a protégé before he knew it.

Even if my father was determined to see me succeed him, I would get a few good years to build my true dream career as a professional chef. I'd just graduated culinary school, I had a great internship at a Michelin-starred restaurant in New York City, and I was ready to go. Dad was healthy, he adored his company, and loved his work, so why would he retire?

The heart attack had other plans.

I'll never forget Mom's voice when I picked up the

phone and heard her sobbing uncontrollably. She and Dad loved each other, a really fucking fairytale insane kind of love, and while I miss Dad, I think what hurts me more than losing my father is seeing what losing her husband did to my mother.

It was Dad's dying wish that I take over for him. He begged Mom to tell me to step up and help with everything. So, I did. How could I say no? Five years down the line and I swear I'm going to lose my fucking mind if I have to step into that office one more time, so. Here we are. Making my mother think I've cracked it because I'm renovating my house.

On my own.

All right, not entirely on my own. I still have a contractor and various work people I've hired. I know when I need to give up and hire an expert. But there's so much I can do by myself, and I've missed working with my hands. It's not the same thing as cooking and baking, which is my real passion, but it still feels good to build something tangible.

Dad got a kick out of business and finances. He loved the business, loved traveling to locations and scouting places to build a new resort, and loved staying in his hotels incognito with Mom to test them out. He cared about the company.

That's not what fulfills me, but I have to carry on his legacy. I owe it to him and to my mother. And so here we are, doing construction on my own home.

I enjoy learning new things and working with hands, but unfortunately, I can't just abandon my father's company, so I have to do it when I'm not at work, usually early in the morning and then later in the evening.

Nobody's had a problem with it so far. Our houses are

pretty damn far apart so I don't think anyone can overhear what I'm up to, and I hop up early and get right to work hammering and sawing away.

"Hey!"

I frown, pausing. Did I just hear someone?

"Hey, you! Yeah, you, dumbass with the saw!"

Okay, someone's definitely yelling at me. I put down my tools and look around for the source of the voice. It seems to be coming from my front gate. I head down there, and find there's a young woman standing in front of my gate.

I'll be honest, my first thought is that she's gorgeous. My second thought is oh, she's angry. Her dark blonde hair is tied up behind her head, and there's an expression of absolute *fury* on her face. I have to admit, it's kind of hot to see her all riled up. I appreciate a woman who goes after what she wants. It's just that what she seems to want right now is to rip my head off.

I politely use the buzzer to open the gate for her. "Can I help you?"

Fuck, she is beautiful. She's got these bright blue eyes with long lashes and a mouth that looks like it was made for smirking. She's only wearing a tank top and what looks like pajama shorts; it's hard for me to keep my eyes on her face. Any other time, I'd be asking to buy her a drink, but I have the feeling if I ask her if she'd like a coffee, she'd accept just to throw it in my face.

"Are you out of your damn mind? You're doing *construction* at a god-awful hour of the morning. Do you have no consideration for your neighbors?" the woman snaps at me. "What are you even—is this a barn? Are you building a barn?"

She's looking over my shoulder at my house. And, yes, I opted for a rustic look, but calling it a *barn*... "Bold of you to talk, you're reliving the colonial era if you're the house right over that hedge there. George Washington called; he wants his pillars back."

"The Amish called, they want their barn back," the woman snaps back at me.

I fold my arms. "Who the hell even are you? You've been here for how many months while I've been working on this, and you've had no problem with me."

"Of course Chloe never said anything." The woman rolls her eyes. "Chloe would sleep through the end of the world, and she probably wasn't home half the time anyway."

She makes a face, like she probably shouldn't have said that. Well, if she's regretting what she's said to me, it's too late for that. "This is still my property, and I can do what I want on it."

"And I'm still living next door to you, being woken up at five in the morning!" She folds her arms. "Do you really have nothing better to do? I'm sorry if your wealth has given you a complex, and you're starting your midlife crisis early, but stop making it my problem."

"Midlife crisis? Just how old do you think I am? And how old are you, are you even old enough to drink?"

The woman's jaw drops open. "Wow. And here I thought women were only insulted for looking too old; now you're breaking the stereotypes and being offensive in a completely new way!"

"And you're sure breaking stereotypes, I thought only teenage boys with too much time on their hands climbed into people's backyards."

"I know a stereotype I'll break next, showing you I know how to use power tools by demonstrating on your face."

"And I'll show you a revolutionary device called calling the cops and having you taken in for trespassing."

The woman's phone beeps; she looks like she literally wants to strangle me with frustration. "I don't have time for this. Just—learn some consideration!"

She storms off through my yard to the front gate. I get the feeling if she could slam it shut behind her, she would. Jeez. What the fuck? I admit, I like watching her walk away, she's got a great ass—but there goes any of the Zen I was working on for today.

I pull out my phone and call my assistant Nadia. "Hey, N, I'm not going to come into the office today."

"But—Simon, you have interviews today, remember?"

Ah, shit. Nadia's going on maternity leave which means I need a new assistant. I'll be honest I'm not super happy about it, but I'm not going to force Nadia to work when she's pregnant and has an infant. She deserves to spend time with her child. That's more important than any job.

"You know more about the job than I do, N, you live it. I trust you to interview the applicants and pick someone who will work well with me."

"It's important for you to meet them too, Simon. I'm not you. I might like someone and you end up disagreeing."

"N, you've been helping run my business and my life for five years now, so I'm pretty sure you know more about me than I even do. You know my blood type and my coffee order and where my social security card is."

"I could probably steal your identity and nobody would notice," Nadia agrees cheerfully.

"See? It'll be fine. I really want to keep working on these home improvements, and my neighbor just ruined my morning, I guess she's got a bee up her ass or something."

"Well... you don't really have anything else on the

agenda, so if you really want me to handle it, I can. It might be good for me to start training whoever she ends up being without you there, so we're not throwing her into the deep end."

"I'm following your lead, N, nobody knows this job better than you. And thank you. I really... I need to get out of that damn office."

"Of course, Simon. Talk later."

I sigh down at my phone as she hangs up. I really wouldn't be anywhere without Nadia. I wouldn't admit it since I'm technically her boss, but she might be my best friend. And even if I wasn't her boss I couldn't ever tell her because she'd never let me forget it.

I am grateful for the day out of the office, though. That argument with my next-door neighbor was jarring, and as much as a part of me... got a thrill fighting with her... the last thing I want to do after that is go to work and deal with a bunch of idiots, stuck in that office.

Nadia can definitely handle it. I know what I want in an assistant, and it's Nadia. So why wouldn't she be good at figuring out who would replace her? It's not a problem.

I have a house to remodel. And the woman next door can just deal with it, cute ass or not.

Chapter 3

Rose

I manage to get to my interview on time, even though I'm completely frazzled from my argument with Chloe's neighbor. Of course, the man I'm willing to storm over to yell at has to be handsome as sin, his dark hair sticking to his face with sweat and his shirt clinging to his muscles, showing off just how buff his arms and chest are. I felt like I was losing my mind when I got a good look at him.

Is he a model? Or an actor? It would make sense since he can afford to live in that neighborhood. And now I've gone and ruined our relationship by yelling at him. Except, hold on, why would I care if he's hot? He was hammering away at five in the morning! What kind of lunatic does that? And he didn't want to apologize, either. He acted like I was crazy for being upset. Screw him.

The place I'm interviewing at is this gorgeous office in Beverly Hills. I'm a little surprised they're not downtown, but given that it's a company about giving people a luxury vacation, I think the founder felt that putting it in a luxury neighborhood helped sell the idea.

When I get to the lobby, I'm greeted by a slightly older woman who's visibly pregnant. "Rose Faraday?"

"Yes, hi, that's me." I stand and shake her hand. "You must be Nadia."

"Good guess. I'm actually also the person you'll be replacing. If you'll follow me, we'll be conducting the interview in Mr. Chaucer's office."

"He's not in today?"

"No, he asked me to handle the hiring process for the applicants since you'll be replacing me. He didn't want you to feel intimidated by him... breathing over your shoulder, so to speak."

Odd, but hopefully that means he'll have a more relaxed attitude in general when it comes to being my boss. "Well, if anyone knows what the job requires it's you."

Nadia smiles. "Thank you. I like to think so."

We get into the elevator and ride it to the top floor. "I've worked for Mr. Chaucer for the last five years. He's an excellent boss to work for, but as CEO he has a demanding schedule. One of your biggest jobs will be keeping track of his meetings and emails so that no paperwork gets lost or meetings get missed."

"Of course."

The elevator doors open and Nadia leads me out into the floor. "Mr. Chaucer is a good boss to work for, but one thing you'll find is that he isn't about the daily grind. He's not someone whose entire life is work, and he'll respect that it's the same for you. However, sometimes things do come up outside of normal work hours, so just keep your phone handy in case you get a late email. Chances are, though, if you don't want to answer it, neither does Mr. Chaucer, so you should be fine. Once five p.m. hits, he doesn't want to do work any more than you do."

"Doesn't sound like most CEOs I know," I blurt out before I can stop myself.

Nadia laughs. "He's not, and that's a good thing."

"I take it you're leaving because of the baby?"

Nadia nods, leading me into a large office of glass and chrome, with a nameplate of *C.E.O.* on the door. "Yes. Mr. Chaucer insisted I get maternity leave not just for my pregnancy but the entire first year after my child's born. I like my job and I'll miss it, but I appreciate his generosity and support. But it does mean we can't make do just with a temp, we need someone official."

"And that's where I come in." I hope I don't sound over-confident.

"Hopefully." Nadia smiles and sits down. "So, let's talk about your past experience."

I feel really good about the interview. I like Nadia, and Mr. Chaucer sounds like a good man. It really reassures me to know he appreciates Nadia so much and is looking after her while she has her baby. I don't plan on getting pregnant right now, but I want to be a mother, someday.

Nadia did warn me that Mr. Chaucer can be stubborn and set in his ways, but I'm sure I can handle that. This is too good an opportunity to pass up.

I'm excited to get home and make something in Chloe's massive, gorgeous kitchen, but when I pull into the driveway, I find that the damn construction is still going on.

Okay, hell no. That's it. I march up to the front gate this time, hitting the buzzer repeatedly. There's no answer, not that I expected much of one. Well, fine. These hedges look pretty climbable. I take off my heels that I wore for the job interview, remove my jacket, roll up the sleeves of my blouse, and get to work.

The hedges are more than I bargained for, without as many solid footholds as I expected, but I manage to get up and over them. I nearly fall a couple of times, but I jump down without breaking anything.

Now to deal with the jerk.

He's still working on an open section of the house, playing music now, too, and there's no way I'm putting up with this for the rest of my night. I storm over. "Hey! You haven't tired yourself out by now? Shot yourself in the foot with a nail gun?"

The man nearly drops his hammer as he stares at me, his mouth open a little in shock, and that's when it hits me that he's shirtless.

Oh, God. If he was hot before with his shirt on, it's even worse now, his broad chest and firm body gleaming in the light from the afternoon sun. I stutter, staring at him like an idiot.

"You again?" the man says, and oh, yeah, I hate him. He might be handsome, but that probably means he's the kind of guy who's used to getting everything he wants because nobody says no to him.

"Yeah. Me again. You want to knock it off? Some of us actually went to work today and want to relax."

The man snorts and shakes his head at me, smirking. "You're impossible. You can't just mind your own business?"

"I'll mind my own business when your business doesn't interrupt mine. Give it a rest! Or I'll register a noise complaint."

The guy steps up to me, frowning. "Oh, yeah, a noise

complaint, that's really going to burst my bubble, sweetheart."

"I'm not your sweetheart," I snap. "And put a damn shirt on."

"Oh, I'm sorry, am I distracting you?" he asks and smirks.

"I suppose you don't care about sunburn, then," I snap. "That's fine by me. Just let me eat my dinner in peace, okay?"

"What is your problem? Seriously. This is my house and my property, not yours."

"And what is *your* problem with being unable to just keep to normal hours? You didn't have to start so damn early in the morning, and you're still at it? I need some peace and quiet at some point."

"Not my fault you can't just put on some headphones and keep out of my yard. Did you climb a damn hedge to get in here? That says a lot more about you than it does about me, sweetheart."

"I *said*," I snap, getting right up in his face, "I'm not your sweetheart. We have a damn app." I hold up my phone. "You couldn't just have sent a warning you'd be doing construction? You couldn't wait until, what, seven at least?"

"And you couldn't just stay off my property?"

I poke him in the chest. "You couldn't answer your damn buzzer?"

"You couldn't have used the app yourself?"

"You couldn't just think about your neighbors? And put a shirt on!"

"Why is it bothering you so much that I'm not wearing a shirt?" He steps in closer, smirking, and I swallow hard. "Is it... distracting you? That's the second time you've brought it up. Unless you really care so much about skin cancer."

"Maybe I had a relative die from skin cancer. You don't know."

"No, I do know. I know you're trying to still look me in the eyes and not at my chest."

"Oh, like you weren't trying not to ogle my breasts this morning. I saw you, you weren't subtle."

"What can I say? You're hot when you're angry."

"Oh, good, because right now? I'm *furious*." I push him in the chest to make him stumble back a little, but the guy doesn't move. Holy shit, he's strong. I try not to blush, but I can feel the heat crawling up my face, and I know I'm not succeeding.

"I knew this neighborhood might have some real spoiled pricks in it but I didn't think I'd have to actually *deal* with them. You take entitlement to a whole new level."

The guy snorts. "You fit right in here, babe, I hate to tell you. Actually, wait, no, I don't hate to tell you. You climbed over my goddamn hedge so you could give me a piece of your mind, and you want to talk about who's entitled here? You can't just order people around and tell them what to do. And I should know, it's literally my job."

"Oh of course. I should've guessed. You're, what, some hedge fund manager or oil baron's kid? You just get to tell people what to do, but I bet you've never had to actually work a day in your life."

"You don't know me," the man growls, and oh, now I've made him actually angry. "Don't pretend you have any idea who I am."

"Then don't pretend you have any idea who I am," I snap back at him.

We're standing only an inch apart, glaring at each other, and my heart is pounding. I feel like I'm going to crawl out of my skin with frustration. I need to do something, anything, to deal with this tension and fury that's building inside of me.

The man's dark eyes are blazing at me, like he can see right through me. I feel a spark run through my body that I haven't experienced in... years, or possibly ever. I inhale sharply, watching him watch me, feeling that connection—

The next thing I know, we're kissing.

He grabs me and hauls me against him, and oh fuck, he's already half-hard. I gasp in surprise and pleasure. It's been so long since I was with anyone, felt anything other than the touch of my own hand, and I grab onto his shoulders, panting as he slides his tongue into my mouth and his arm wraps around my waist.

I bite at him, not willing to give in so easily, even in a kiss, but that doesn't seem to bother him at all. He kisses me just as ferociously right back. My hands slide over his chest, feeling the muscles shifting and pressing up under my touch. Fuck, he's strong and built, and his warm skin against my fingers makes me feel insane. I want to drive him crazy. I feel competitive, angry, out of control. If I can't win this argument verbally, then I feel like I have to win it another way, I have to make him come undone for me.

I drop to my knees, letting the fire in my stomach and my impulse carry me, as I hurry to undo his pants. He gasps down at me, chest heaving, a look of shock on his face. I smirk up at him. Yeah, I've got him now.

"Rose," I tell him. "Just so you know what name to say."

The guy snorts. "Simon," he fires back. "So you know what name to scream."

Yeah, right. No guy's gotten me to scream during sex yet. I don't think Simon here is going to be the one to change that, but I'll worry about that later. Right now I'm focused on pulling his hard, hot cock out and getting my mouth on it.

Fuck, he's thick, and my mouth waters. My body pulses with desire. It's been way too long since I had sex or even really found time to be seriously attracted to someone. I've been too busy trying to keep my head above water. This has to be why I'm so attracted to Simon, and why my anger has morphed into sex. It's just been a long time, that's all.

Simon's hands slide into my hair as I tease him, getting my tongue on him. I want him to be blown away, I want him to give in and concede defeat in one way if not another. I want him to give me what I want and I want to feel like I've won something. And oh, fuck, it really helps that he's hot.

I haven't done this in forever, but I feel almost caught up in an ocean of desire, drowning in how much I want to have him in my mouth. I lick all over, indulging, reminding myself what this feels like and how I like to do it, how much I enjoy it. Simon gapes down at me, like he can't quite believe this is happening. I swirl my tongue around the tip of his cock, watching him jolt and try to hold his hips in place, and then wink at him right before I sink my mouth down onto him.

I let my eyes fall closed as I bob my head up and down, falling into the rhythm of it. My hands wrap around Simon's muscled thighs and shiver as his fingers tighten in my hair. It's making me so fucking wet, feeling him in my mouth heavy on my tongue, stretching out my jaw.

Simon pants above me, slowly hitching his hips up into my mouth, and it's intoxicating. I forgot how much I enjoyed this and how good it would make me feel. I speed up a bit, swirling my tongue, dragging it along the underside of the shaft, teasing the head. I want to make him break the way he wouldn't when we argued.

Simon groans quietly, and I resist the urge to grin with triumph, tasting the salt of his precum on my tongue. He's close, I can feel it in the way he twitches and jerks in my mouth. I'm sure I can make him orgasm, I'm sure—but he doesn't give in. Instead, he yanks me carefully off, and cups my chin in his hand, tilting my face up.

The look on his face has me so wet, I almost moan.

"Oh, we're not done yet," he growls. "I'm *far* from finished with you."

My mouth goes dry and heat shoots through me, the look in his eyes a dark, heady promise.

I may be in for more than I bargained for.

Chapter 4

Simon

I don't know which one of us kisses each other first, but that's just the latest surprise when it comes to Rose. When she came striding across my front lawn, I was fucking gobsmacked. How the hell had she gotten in? She had bits of green from the hedge sticking to her; it hit me that she'd climbed over the damn hedge to get in so she could yell at me.

Honestly? I kinda appreciate the determination. I hadn't heard her at the gate, so I guess she decided she wasn't going to let that stop her.

It's been a good day, the morning notwithstanding, and I'm feeling a lot more accomplished and relaxed now. But then Rose is back in my yard yelling at me again, and I just can't handle it.

Or, rather, I can.

The thing is, I think she's probably right. I've just never had my neighbors complain about my weird hours of construction before, so I assumed it was all fine. But it is inconsiderate of me to start so early in the morning or go later into the evening if it actually is something my neighbors can hear and have to deal with. Normally, I would apologize and try to work something out with her, since I have to work around my office schedule. But there's something about Rose's fire that makes me not want to give in. I want to keep pushing her buttons. I want to see how far she can go, how far we can both go with this.

I'm still shocked when she drops to her knees, but in the best way. She's got her mouth on my cock like she's determined to make me come down her throat, and fuck, I appreciate it, it feels amazing. She's determined, her tongue teasing me, and my hands slide into her soft blonde hair without even thinking about it.

I want to tug. I want to hold her still and thrust into her mouth until I come. I want to chase the release I can feel building at the base of my spine. But I also don't want to give her the satisfaction. It's clear that she wants to make me come undone; she wants to win the argument this way, and I'm not about to let her.

I'm going to make her world spin. I'm going to show her just what I can do to a woman. She's going to be screaming my name. I pull Rose back, staring down at her as I struggle to catch my breath. The temptation to slide my cock back into her mouth is strong, but I ignore it. I'm going to do so much more with her. If she thinks that she can just blow me and that means she's 'won' something then she's got another thing coming.

"I'm *far* from finished with you," I promise her.

Rose stares up at me, her lips slick and swollen from being on my cock; her face is flushed, and her lush blonde hair tangles around my fingers. I stare down at her for a moment and it hits me hard that she's truly gorgeous. I want her so fucking badly. I don't know the last time I wanted a woman like this.

Maybe it's just the competitive bastard in me. I've never backed down from a challenge, whether it was the heat and pressure of a professional kitchen or the responsibility of taking over my father's company. I want to show Rose just what she's in for, and just what I can give her.

I'm going to make her damn head spin. She thinks she can wipe my mind just from a blowjob? This sweetheart has another thing coming. I pull Rose to her feet and pick her up. She gasps and wraps her legs around me as I carry her a few feet inside my house.

There is a bit of a mess; there's no way I'm going to let either of us possibly get hurt from a stray piece of construction. I carry her to my spotless kitchen, the very first area of the house I remodeled—the area that's completely clean and spotless—and I set her on the counter.

Rose stares at me in shock, probably at my strength, and I grin at her. "You thought I did all that construction myself and wasn't strong enough to pick you up?"

I draw my nose along the curve of her neck, smiling, inhaling the sweet scent of her. "Oh, baby, you have no idea."

Rose shudders. "Stop talking the talk and walk the walk," she snaps, shoving at me.

I snort and push her lightly down onto the counter. "Not into the foreplay, huh?" I growl.

"Not with *you*," she snaps back.

Oh, if that's how she wants it. I kiss her, hard and dirty, grinding against her so she can remember just how goddamn hard I am. Rose's legs spread instantly, greedily, and I shove her skirt up and her panties to the side.

"Somebody dressed pretty today," I murmur. "Some-where important to be? Trying to impress somebody?"

"Yeah," she pants. "Someone a whole lot nicer than you."

"But not sexier." I kiss the words right out of her mouth so that she can't say anything more. She's going to have to admit that I spin her head around, and I'm going to win this stupid argument. And then, maybe, I'll be magnanimous about the construction. Maybe.

I yank open her blouse, a button flying somewhere, and Rose bites my lip. "You're paying for that!"

"I'll pay for a whole new wardrobe, sweetheart," I promise her. Who cares about one blouse when I can get my hands on her luscious breasts?

Rose gasps as I massage them, tweaking her nipples, and playing with them. The way her body rolls against me is delicious. "Been a while, huh, sweetheart?"

"Oh I'm sure it takes one to know one," Rose pants back at me.

I set my mouth on her skin. "If by 'a while' you mean a week, then yeah, honey, it's been a while for me."

"Bragging about one-night stands isn't the virtue you think it is." Rose's quip doesn't have the right bite when she's gasping under my mouth as I make my way down her body.

Fuck, she's really gorgeous. I want to take my time with her. I would, if she was any other woman. If she was one of my usual hookups. But Rose is far from that. She's not some woman I met in a bar after a long day stuck in the office, looking for something to distract me from work. I'm not here to have *fun*. I'm winning the damn argument and showing her that she can't just mouth off at me and think she can get the upper hand.

This isn't a hookup, it's a competition.

We grab at each other, nearly ripping our clothes as

Rose yanks me back up. I get between her legs, yanking her until her ass is on the very edge of the counter so I can thrust into her. *Fuck*. Fuck she feels amazing.

Rose claws at my shoulders like she's trying to get even closer to me. I'm as deep inside her as I can fucking get, and it's like it still isn't enough for her. I want to make another quip, to joke about how desperate she is, but fuck I'm desperate too. I want her to ruin this with a stupid joke.

All of the anger fades away. Maybe "fades away" isn't the right term; it's more like it's transformed, pushed into this all-consuming lust. I thrust into her hard and fast. Rose continues to claw at me, gasping, arching. I'm giving as good as I'm getting. The wet, tight heat of her makes me feel like I'm insane. I can't remember the last time I was this mind-less over someone.

I'm a damn good lover. I pride myself on it. But right now I'm not thinking about showing off all I can do and all I know. I'm just chasing the high and taking her with me. I'm giving into the *need*, and I'm bringing her with me.

Rose's voice rises in pitch. She sounds almost surprised, like she didn't think she could feel this good this *way*. I get it, for sure. I'm kind of feeling the same way, all of that passion overtaking me in a way I didn't think could happen anymore. I can't remember the last time I felt this overcome by my emotions, chasing it high harder and harder until I felt like I wasn't in control anymore.

I bury my face in her neck as Rose's head falls back. She stops clawing at me, clinging instead, and we fall into some kind of rhythm together, moving as one. Fuck she's so fucking hot, I feel amazing, I feel like I've been falling off a cliff and finally I'm flying. Rose's leg comes up around my waist and I groan, getting my hand up under her ass to lift her hips up. I feel like an animal, lost in the moment completely, as Rose's voice spirals higher and higher.

"S-Simon." She clutches at me, her voice almost a warning. "Simon, I—I'm—oh God—"

I feel her clench down tight around me and come, a rush right to my head. I jerk inside of her, thrusting wildly, and let the pleasure overtake me completely.

Rose slumps back onto the counter and I follow her, the two of us breathing hard. It takes a few seconds for my brain to come back online.

"What the fuck was that?" I ask, still out of breath.

"I—you started it."

"Sure I did."

Rose pinches me and I slide out of her, glaring. "You're the one who climbed into my backyard."

"You're the one who had the construction going and you're the one who kissed me."

"You kissed me," I tell her, but the truth is I'm actually not sure who did what.

"Doesn't matter." Rose reaches around for the paper towels and starts to clean herself up. "It was just hate sex, that's all. Getting the tension out."

"You're absolutely right." I'm relieved to hear her say that. I don't want her thinking that I like her now. Unfortunately, when you have sex with someone, sometimes they think it means more than it does, a deeper relationship than you intend. "It won't happen again."

"The sex, or the construction at annoying hours?"

"I'm sure you can guess." I clean myself up, too. "The door's that way; close the gate after you when you leave. Unless you feel like climbing the hedge again."

Rose glares at me and hops off the counter. "You're insufferable."

"Takes one to know one."

She storms out of the house, and I slump back against the fridge. Goddamn. That was some amazing sex. I haven't let go like that in years—rough and wild. I stop thinking for five damn minutes. Rose is gorgeous, and I almost wish I could ask for another round tomorrow. If only she wasn't the most frustrating woman in the world. Yeah. It's definitely not happening again. No way.

Chapter 5

Rose

My legs shake as I hurry home, my body tingling with the aftershocks from my amazing orgasm and my mind racing in a blur.

I haven't had sex impulsively like that in possibly ever. I can't get over how amazing I felt. Simon fucked me like he'd lost his mind, and I felt like I'd lost mine—like the only thing that was left was passion. I couldn't even remember why I was so damn angry at him; I just knew he made me feel amazing.

I needed that. I'll never, ever admit it to him because God knows he's made it clear he still hates me and isn't going to change his damn construction behavior; but fuck, I needed someone to fuck me hard and wear me out like that. I haven't come so hard in—ever. Fuck.

And, of course, it had to be an asshole like Simon. Dammit. It couldn't have been some charming guy that I bumped into at a coffee shop; it had to be Chloe's annoying asshole neighbor who had me screaming and seeing stars.

I hurry back into the house and hop into the shower. As the aftershocks of my orgasm wind down I feel almost... not

ashamed, no. But embarrassed. Yes. Extremely embarrassed. What came over me? What the hell was I thinking? I
wash off and get ready for bed, then check my email.
There's one from Nadia, telling me that she'd like to offer
me the job, and could I come in for onboarding?

My heart leaps in my chest. I almost burst into tears
from relief. This is a really well-paying job and Chloe won't
be in Europe forever. I need to build up some money to get
my company started, and I should have some money in
savings for when I inevitably move out and get my own
apartment. This job will help me do that.

I respond immediately and collapse back onto the bed. I
can't believe I just had sex with Chloe's neighbor. I can't
believe I just got this job. I don't even know what to call this
day. I do know that I'm staying away from Simon, though.
Fuck him and his construction and his selfish, stubborn attitude. The horrible truth is that it felt amazing to have him
inside of me, fucking me—the way he picked me up so
easily and carried me around, the way he yanked at my
clothes and kissed all over my body frantically... like he
wanted to devour me.

No way am I going near him again. I'm not sure I could
resist temptation, and I don't want him thinking that he can
just have sex with me or kiss me. I'm going to forget just
how rude he is. No way. It was a lapse in judgment, that's
all. It won't happen again. I was angry, I somehow got
carried away, but I can hold onto my self-control now.

Besides, I have a new job to focus on. I'm not going to
waste my time getting into arguments with Chloe's asshole
neighbor, or banging him, no matter how amazing that sex
felt. Yes, it felt good to let go and let my emotions take over.
I feel like I unleashed something inside of myself that had

been bottled up. But the guy's a jerk. I can do so much better than him.

I contact Nadia about the onboarding and spend the next week going into the office to train with her, so I'm ready for my new job. I still don't meet Mr. Chaucer, and I suspect that Nadia doesn't want me to meet him too soon in case I'm intimidated by him. She mentions a few times how stubborn he can be, and I think he probably runs roughshod over a lot of people.

Well, he's not going to intimidate me, whoever he is. I'm going to knock this job out of the park.

I meet a lot of the other people in the office, too, and they're all fine. Nadia takes me to the break room to meet people while we have lunch brought in from the burrito place down the street.

Everyone seems happy to meet me. "I can't believe Nadia's actually leaving," one of the other women tells me.

"You're not married, or dating, are you?" one of the guys jokes. I think his name's Brian, if I'm remembering correctly. "Because the last thing we need is another person going on maternity leave."

"Ah, no, I'm single," I reply.

Definitely the wrong answer. I can feel all the men in the room staring at me now. I resist the urge to roll my eyes. Unlike Chloe's annoying neighbor Simon, I actually do have to deal with these men, and I don't want them pissed at me too quickly. I can just politely refuse any dating offers if they come along.

"Has Nadia filled you in?" another woman asks me. Sabrina. Or Selina?

31

"Yes, she's been showing me how to do everything, she's really helpful."

The woman rolls her eyes. "No, has she filled you in on the latest gossip!"

Oh, God. "Um. No. I don't think that's part of my job description," I joke.

"Well, I'm sure you've noticed that Mr. Chaucer hasn't been around. His father would often go to the resorts to test them out with his wife, a surprise inspection kind of thing? Rumor has it that's what Chaucer is doing now, except with this supermodel—"

Oh boy. My boss is supposedly a womanizer. Well, that's fine, as long as it doesn't affect my ability to do my job, and he doesn't make me schedule his sex. "I'm sorry, I think I have to go..." I say quickly, backing out of the conversation.

I really do not care about who does what in this office. I'm here to keep my head down and stay out of other people's business. I'm going to focus on doing my job. The sooner I can get my career off the ground the better. I won't do that if I get distracted by people talking about who's sleeping with whom in the paper supply closet.

Whatever people get up to is none of my business unless it affects my ability to do my job, and so far I'm not seeing any reason for that to change. But I don't want to make everyone mad, so I just try to escape and follow Nadia along as she continues to mentor me. She doesn't seem to care either, at least, bless her. But I figure having a baby on the way pushes everything else out of your mind.

Still, I'm stressed as hell by the time I get back to Chloe's place. There's so much to learn, and Mr. Chaucer is the CEO of a massive company. I have to get everything right. I keep running over everything in my head, rereading my notes as I get out of the car—only to hear that damn construction going on. Hammering and sawing and banging. Seriously?

It's only six p.m., so I try not to say anything just yet. It's not super late. But the noise just keeps going, until it's nine in the fucking evening. Is he doing it on purpose? He knows I can hear him, it has to be on purpose. Well, if he thinks that I'm going to march over there and give him some more sex and this is his weird way of trying to entice me, then he's got another thing coming. Like hell I'm going over there again.

I pull out my phone instead and get onto the app that Chloe gave me, then make a post. I haven't really looked at the app yet; it's stuff like neighbors saying when they'll be on vacation, reminding others what day is trash day, and things like that. But I just take a screenshot of noise ordinances in HOA neighborhoods and then post the screenshot.

It's passive-aggressive, yeah, but it should get my point across. Maybe if I shame him publicly in front of his neighbors, this guy will back off. I get a few comments that are basically *who are you and what are you talking about,* and then I hear the construction stop.

I smirk and finally start getting ready for bed. But when I pull out my phone again, I have a new comment, from Simon.

Really? Pulling all the other neighbors into this?

I tap out a reply. *You leave me no choice.*

You could've just come on over here again.

Oh, you'd like that, wouldn't you? Here, I'll do that, let me just grab a baseball bat.

Such violence. This comment is accompanied by a link to a 24-Hour Fitness and a martial arts studio. The implication is pretty clear—he thinks I should work off my anger by exercising.

Ha. Ha. Ha.

That's when we get a few other comments. *Uh, guys? What's going on here?*

Hey, could you two just text like normal people?

Guys leave us out of this.

I roll my eyes and go to toss my phone away. At least the damn construction noises have stopped, and that's what matters. I have to get up in the morning. I'm already so wound up that I'll probably have to take melatonin or something to get to sleep.

But then my phone dings with one more comment from Simon. It's his number. I type it in. This is stupid. It's so stupid. I should ignore him. But I can't let him have the last word and brand me a coward. I type his number in and save it on my phone, and then I text him.

You really have a humiliation kink or something?

His response is immediate. *You're the one who started this so I think I should be asking you that question. Although you did seem to like praise the other night.*

Oh, fuck you.

You already did that. You blew me, too.

Sorry, that part was so boring and unmemorable that I forgot about it.

Silly me, and here I was combing my hair in front of the mirror and feeling pretty and special.

The sarcasm is practically dripping from my phone at that last sentence he sends. I grit my teeth. *If you wanted to feel special and pretty then maybe you should stop the damn construction. Unless it was your pathetic attempt to get me to come over again, in which case, congratulations! You are offi-*

cially the most desperate guy and the worst flirter I've ever met.

There's no response for a moment. I settle into bed, propped up against the pillows. For some reason, I find myself... feeling disappointed at the lack of response. Which is stupid and silly. I want the guy to leave me alone.

...right?

My phone buzzes with another text before I can let myself think too hard about it. *Honey, if I wanted to see you again, I wouldn't be doing construction and just hoping that would get you over here. I'd come over there to you. When I want something, I go after it.*

My mouth goes dry. *Good thing you don't want me, then.*

Who said I didn't?

Oh, so you're outside my front door right now?

Well, no, see I was a little worried you'd have that base- ball bat swinging the second I rang the doorbell.

Coward.

Is that your way of saying you want me to come over?

I'm not saying that. But even as I tell myself that, I realize I'm flushed, and my breath is coming in faster. I don't want Simon to come over. I don't want to have sex with him again.

My thighs press together, and I swallow hard. The memory of his hot, thick cock inside of me—fucking me in a way I've only ever imagined and never actually experienced. It was the kind of wild amazing fucking you think doesn't really happen because when you try to have it at nightclubs or bars or wherever, it just ends up being disappointing. The guy gets his and the girl doesn't, and you feel like a piece of meat.

But not last night. Dammit.

I ponder what to say. I want it. I don't want it. I want it. I don't... My phone lights up. *Not that I'd never come over to get you off.* I snort at his blatant confidence, but also... I don't know; it feels kind of like he's also going out on a limb here, putting himself out there a little more. Maybe I'm just giving him too much credit, but I want to reward him for that.

Yeah, right.

Don't believe me?

I'll believe it when it actually happens.

As if you haven't been thinking about me since the other night. As if you haven't replayed over and over how my cock felt inside of you. Do you want that again? Because I don't think I'd go so fast this time. I think I'd hold your legs open, keep the angle so it's not hitting your sweet spot, and then fuck you as you sob on the edge of orgasm. Until you're begging me to let you come.

My entire body goes hot. I feel like I can almost sense him inside of me again. I swallow hard. *Who says I'd beg for you?*

Everything about you. You know, I didn't return the favor yesterday. That was rude of me. I should put my mouth on you, first. Or maybe after. I left such a mess... maybe I should clean it up with my tongue this time.

My hand slides down my legs, teasing myself. I don't touch myself properly, but the temptation is there. It's so strong I can taste it.

I text him back one-handed. *Maybe I should ride you this time and show you how I like it.*

I know how you like it. You loved it when I picked you up and carried you. You liked how I could put you exactly where I wanted you.

I swallow hard. That's not... *not* true.

A thought occurs to me as my fingers trace up and down my thigh, and I text him, *are you touching yourself?*

Do you want me to be?

I refuse to let this guy have the upper hand this entire time. If he wants to dirty talk, then damn it, so can I. *I'm touching myself. Sliding my fingers up and down... getting them so wet... I bet you wish you could watch.*

There's a minute with no response. Maybe I've just ruined things. I shakily start to type out an apology, my heart in my throat, but then my phone lights up—not with a text, but with a call.

Simon's calling me.

Chapter 6

Simon

When I saw the post on the app from Rose, I knew that it was about me. It was late, later than I had realized. I lose track of time when I'm lost in a project. I stop the construction for the night, wrap things up, and head inside to take a quick shower and make myself something to eat.

I can't resist needling Rose a bit. I can't let her just make a public post like that and think she can get away with it, assuming I won't say anything or retaliate in any way. Our comments quickly annoy our neighbors, and while I might act like I don't care to Rose, I don't actually want my neighbors reporting me or showing up on my front lawn because I was blowing up their phones arguing with the new girl on the block, so I give her my number.

To my surprise, she actually texts me. I wasn't sure she would. It's not like she really *wants* to talk to me. She just wants me to stop bugging her with the noise. But maybe she's just that competitive and wants to win our little argument decisively. Or maybe, like me, she can't stop thinking about the other night. What it felt like.

I know I can't. I should, I really should. One woman isn't going to turn my head, or so I keep telling myself. But time and again my thoughts keep returning to Rose. The way she smelled, the way she looked, the way she sounded, the way she felt. The memory of her mouth on my cock, her body against mine, and the way she came around me keeps popping into my head. I haven't been able to shake her from my mind.

Maybe she's got a point. I was doing construction just to fuck with her, in the vain hope that she'd find a way to barge into my front yard again. But she didn't. She made a snarky post on the app, and now here we are, texting.

Sexting, really.

When she asks me if I'm touching myself, I can't help it anymore. I'm not, but I want to, my cock hard and aching between my legs as I lean back against my bathroom sink and stare down at the phone. I can imagine her so clearly on the other side, but imagination isn't enough. I need more. I need to hear her.

So I call.

Part of me doesn't think she'll pick up. This is all just some game for her, and she won't actually want to do anything with me again, right? But she does. She fucking *does*, and it sends a thrill through me like a fucking electric shock. I haven't felt this damn invigorated since... since...

Since I had to give up my dream of being a professional chef, honestly.

"Couldn't resist, huh?" Her breathlessness gives her away, but she's trying to hide it. I grin.

"Neither could you." I finally, *finally* reach down and push my pants off, wrapping a hand around my aching cock. "Touching yourself while texting me, you naughty girl. I knew you'd be thinking about what happened. You should've come back over."

Rose snorts. "Fat chance. It's your turn. If you wanted something you should've come over yourself and made good on those promises. Or are you a man who only *talks* about going after what he wants?"

I'm tempted to show her just what I can do, and march over there to bang her door down and fuck her in the foyer of her home. But I just fumble for some lotion from the counter instead and then start stroking my cock, nice and slow.

"I already have what I want," I tell her. "Your voice in my ear, and your pretty little fingers stroking yourself for me. Unless you were lying about that and *you're* the one who's all talk."

"I—" She pauses, and I hear the hitch in her breath. When she speaks again, her voice is a little softer. "I'm not all talk."

"Good. Neither am I."

I bring the phone down so that it's close enough that she can hear my hand moving slowly up and down my cock. I pull the phone back and put it on speaker so I can still hear her and talk to her when both my hands become occupied— or when I just get so overwhelmed I'll be in danger of dropping the damn thing.

I can hear her shaky breathing, and then... the slick sounds of her touching herself.

I groan. "Tell me what you're doing, sweetheart. Narrate it for me."

Rose swallows hard, I can hear it through the phone. "I...."

Silence reigns on the other end. I want to ask if she's ever had phone sex before, maybe make a joke, but I don't like to make fun of the inexperience of my partners. Nobody likes to feel like they're bad or wrong for not being kinky enough during sex. She's doing it now, with me, and that's what matters. It's kinda sexy, actually, if I'm the only person she's done this with.

"I'm stroking my cock nice and slow," I tell her. "Not going too fast, not yet. Nothing fancy. Just keeping myself hard and slick, thinking about you. Thinking about what I want to do to you. I definitely want to get my mouth on you, sweetheart. Before or after I fuck you, doesn't matter. Hell, maybe I'll even do both. You'll be sobbing through your last orgasm by the time I'm through with you."

Rose moans; it's the most fucking delicious sound in the world. "I—I have—I wasn't touching myself before, just on my thigh, I was teasing myself, but now I'm—I'm rubbing my clit—"

"Yeah, that's a good girl."

It's funny. I've been stuck in a lot of stupid meetings the last few days; and when the other people in my company get uppity with me, it just drives me insane. I hate it. It makes me worry that I'm not doing as good of a job as Dad did. I am angry all over again; it reminds me why I hate this job so much, and why I never wanted it. But when Rose gets uppity with me, when she challenges me and argues with me, it just makes me that much hotter under the collar. It turns me on. It makes me feel alive.

All this construction, all these attempts to find some kind of release, Zen, or whatever you want to call it, and I'm finding it by arguing with a woman I just met. And fucking her.

"Can you slide a finger inside for me?" I ask. "I want to fuck you so badly, but I want you nice and open for me first."

41

Rose whines. "Is that what you'd do if you were here?"

"I said I'd take my time, didn't I? No quick wham bam thank you ma'am this time. I want you begging for me. So yeah, I'd finger you, just the one to start out with, nice and slow."

I hear her do it, oh holy fuck I can hear her do it, and I speed up my hand a little. "Yeah, that's it. That's the sound I want to hear."

She could ignore me. She could add another finger, even a third, and get herself off. She could tell me to go screw myself and come, or she could argue and say we're doing things a different way.

For all our fighting, the moment we're actually being sexual together, she follows my lead. It's intoxicating. It's like I have to earn her submission but once I get it, I'm golden. I want to keep earning it, again and again.

I listen to her touching herself, and it takes a hell of a lot in me to not push myself over the edge—not to go too far and too fast on my end. I squeeze the base of my cock now and again, tugging lightly on my balls with my other hand, to keep my own orgasm from drawing too close.

"You want a second finger?" I ask her. I want her to add a second finger, I want it so badly I can taste it on the back of my tongue, but I've got a damn point to make here.

"Y-yes," Rose admits in a whisper.

"It's such a tease, just one finger, isn't it? And yours aren't even as large as mine, so it's even worse. Poor sweetheart. You need it so badly."

Rose whimpers. I grin. "Go ahead. A second finger, that's a good girl for me."

I hear her let out a little moan as she does as she's asked. Fuck, the slick noises of her touching herself through the phone have me feeling dizzy with lust. "Yeah, that's it. That's it."

Rose's breathing is heavy and fast. "Simon—Simon *please* can I add a third?"

"Now, why would I let you do that? Hmm? Are you that desperate to orgasm?"

"N-no, I..." I can feel her embarrassment through the phone. I'm about to find something to say to reassure her, but then she adds, "I want to imagine it's your cock, and I—I need more."

Oh, holy fuck. She's going to kill me. "Go ahead. Imagine that's my cock sliding inside of you. I'm through teasing. You can hear it, can't you? Through the phone? How fast I'm stroking myself? That's how fast I'm going to fuck you. I want you to match my strokes, go on."

Rose moans, louder this time, unashamed; fuck if that doesn't have my cock jolting with need. "Yeah, yeah, yeah," I encourage her. "Let it all out, sweetheart, don't be ashamed. I want to hear it all."

She's fucking herself hard and fast now. I can picture it so clearly, the flush on her face spreading down her throat to her chest, her breasts heaving, her blue eyes open and glassy with desire, her lips bitten red and slick. God, she's fucking gorgeous.

"I'm going to fuck you until you scream," I promise her. "You screamed for me before but I know I can get you louder this time, more desperate this time. Can you hear me? I want you to hear me, I want you to know what you do to me..."

"Simon." Rose's voice is cracking. "Simon, please, can I —I want to come, I want—please let me come, oh my God please let me come, I'm close but I—please—"

It feels like someone's punched me in the gut, but in the

best way possible. She's holding off her orgasm for me. She's waiting for me to tell her she can. There's no holding back at that. I fumble for the tissues and manage to grab them just in time to spill into them, coming hard, my toes curling. Holy *fuck*.

"Yes," I blurt out. "Yes, come for me, come on. I'm going to let you come. Rub that clit for me and fuck yourself on your fingers, that's a good girl. Pretend it's me fucking you, I'd fuck you so goddamn good if I was there right now—"

"Oh my God," Rose babbles. "Oh my God, Simon, *Simon...*"

She lets out a little cry and I hear her coming, my cock twitching and giving a weak pulse at the noise and the image in my head.

She's got to look so goddamn gorgeous right now. Holy shit.

I breathe hard through my nose as the both of us come down from it. I'm tempted to march over to her place right now, but I'm not sure if that would be welcome. Maybe we should just... chat for a minute like this and then leave it at that.

Before I can even truly process what I want to say, though, I hear Rose say abruptly, "Goodnight, Simon."

And the woman hangs up the damn phone!

Chapter 7

Rose

To say that I'm horribly embarrassed would be an understatement.

I grew up helping my father in a warehouse; I've heard the jokes that men make. The whole idea of "'post-nut clarity" and all that. I never really thought about it much. If you asked me, nothing should turn you on so much that you couldn't make a rational decision.

Yet, there I was, still so horny for Simon, and I couldn't even acknowledge it. I had to go and make that post that everyone in our neighborhood saw. Fuck, they must all be talking about us right now. I hope that nobody realizes that there's a flirtatious element to it; otherwise, I can never show my face around here again. Hopefully, they just think it's a weird rivalry, but even people knowing about that is bad enough.

Then we had phone sex. Simon and I had phone sex. I was begging him to let me come, fingering myself while picturing him, pretending it was him, *wishing* it was him.

I'm so fucking screwed.

I hang up the phone and try to go to sleep. I definitely

also try not to think about Simon. The orgasm helps to drop me directly off in dreamland, but the moment I wake up again, of course, I'm right back to thinking about him.

Literally, I wake up and I think, *I wish we'd been on a video call last night.*

Oh my God... what the hell is wrong with me?

I need to get my head on straight. I have way too much going on right now to let myself be distracted by a guy I can't seem to stop fighting or fucking. My head feels like it's turned backward.

I get out of bed and get ready, thankful it's Saturday, and I don't have to go to work. I meet my boss for the first time on Monday. I'd like to make a good impression, and there's no way I could do that if I had to meet him this morning. I have to find some way to get my head on straight with this whole Simon thing before I go crazy.

He must be so proud of himself for getting me to do something sexual with him last night, and I basically begged him to do it. All my protesting and I was so easy... he's going to start up that stupid construction any minute now just to rub it in my face.

After I shower and get dressed for the day, I realize there's no noise. Nothing. It's quiet.

Huh.

I go to make breakfast when I hear the doorbell ring. I hope it's not a package that Chloe forgot to tell me about. Knowing her she probably has something scheduled that she forgot to cancel, and she just forgot to mention it. I hurry to the door. "Coming!"

Simon smiles at me as I open it. I nearly slam the door in his face out of startled instinct. My eyes go wide, I can feel it, and heat crawls up my neck. God, I hope I don't look as shocked as I feel. "Simon?"

He holds up something for me, and I see it's a plate of cookies. "I thought that I would bring these over. As a truce."

I look down at them. He could've possibly taken them out of a box and put them on the plate... but no, I can smell them, fresh out of the oven. "Did you make these?"

"I can do something other than wield a hammer, y'know."

"Oh, I'm sure." I glance back up at him, then at the cookies, then back up at him. "You want a truce?"

"That's why I'm here."

He could be trying something to trick me and drive me even crazier, but he sounds sincere and weirdly, I believe him.

I step back and let him inside. "We can put these in the kitchen."

When we get there I pour him a glass of water. "You want coffee? I was just about to make some."

"That'd be great, thanks."

"Took me forever to figure out this fancy thing." I start up Chloe's fancy coffee maker.

"You just got it?"

"It's not mine. I'm house-sitting for my cousin. I don't live here."

"That explains why I never got any complaints until now. I thought you must've just moved in but I would've heard if someone new was coming."

"Yup. Chloe's off in Europe with her latest boy toy. Don't ask, I don't want to know so I didn't."

Simon grins at me and pushes the plate of cookies my way. "Try one."

"This feels like a lot of effort to go to just to poison me." I take a cookie and bite into it—and make a horribly embarrassing noise. Holy *fuck*. "That's delicious."

Simon looks pleased. Really, genuinely pleased, not at all in a smug way. "I'm really glad to hear it."

"I had no idea you could bake. I mean, I know I don't really know a lot about you, but..."

"I didn't seem the type?"

"Not really, no."

"The construction work is a newer hobby. I need something to do with my hands before I went crazy, and the house needed remodeling when I bought it. Originally, I was going to turn it into my dream house with an actual team, you know, but I figured I could do so much of it myself, why not? The project will take a little longer, but I think it'll be more satisfying at the end of the day."

"You should stick to baking. Seriously, this is amazing." These cookies are like salted caramel chocolate chip. I want to devour the entire plate. "Was this just a hobby you picked up a while ago, or...?"

"I actually was a professional chef," Simon admits.

The coffee machine beeps and I get out some mugs. "Wait, really?"

Maybe he's some celebrity chef and I just didn't recognize him? I don't make a habit of watching reality cooking shows or things like that. But how else would he get the money to afford to live here?

"Yup. I had to give it up a few years ago to run the family business. But that was my passion."

"I get that. My family's angry that I didn't give up my passion to help run their family business."

Although, I'm sure that unlike my father's business, this "family business" that Simon's talking about has to be a hedge fund company or a film studio, something crazy expensive that lets you be a billionaire.

"I'm glad you stuck to your guns on that. Good for you. What are you interested in?"

"Fashion. I always have been." I pour his coffee. "Milk? Sugar?"

"One sugar and just a touch of milk, please."

"You actually said please! He does have manners!" I fix his coffee and pass it to him.

"And you're being a gracious hostess, who knew you had it in you?" There's no bite to Simon's tone. Our fingers brush as I hand him the coffee; I can feel my face heating up.

"Any particular cuisine you liked?" I blurt out, scrambling to cover my reaction.

"I loved a lot of different cuisines. I'm a big fan of fusion food, too, combining one culture with another and seeing what sticks, and how they can blend. I have to say I think Mexican is my favorite, though. Soft spot after growing up in Los Angeles, after all."

"What kind of chef were you?"

"I was starting out so I didn't really have my own place. I was an apprentice sous chef at a place in New York City, but I dreamed of eventually running my own place."

"That's what I want to do, run my own place, except as a clothing store."

"Your designs, or another's?"

"Mine."

"Admirable."

"Thank you." I grimace over my coffee mug. "If I could actually get the damn thing off the ground. I'm struggling to find investors."

"Have you considered starting your brand online only, through social media? You won't have to pay for anything, even a website, and you can control the amount of items you make. You can do one at a time, make one-offs or bespoke items, so you're not overwhelmed trying to create an inventory."

"Huh." That's a good idea. "Are you in a marketing firm?"

"Nope. But I grew up in business." Simon winks at me and finishes his coffee. "I like to think I picked up a thing or two even though it's not my favorite. Anyone who wants to start their own business, no matter what kind, needs to do research on it. No study agrees, but anywhere from sixty to eighty percent of restaurants go under within five years. That's if they make it past the first year, which is the hardest. They have a higher rate of closures than just about any other small business."

"Oof. Any reason why that is?" I'm genuinely interested in this other side of Simon—this smart and educated person who can banter with me and gives me helpful advice just to be nice.

"Well, you have the option to go online only. To make small batches or one-offs. I think social media should really work in your favor. But restaurants need a brick-and-mortar institution, even if it's just to make the food. That's why a lot of people try to start instead with food trucks. The amount you have to invest in a restaurant not just to get it started but to keep it running is immense."

"Fascinating." I mean it when I say that.

Simon grins, but almost bashfully, like he hasn't had anyone show a real interest in all this in some time. "It is. My father never wanted me to become a chef, but he did appreciate the challenge I'd set for myself and the business savviness I'd have to show. He could appreciate that ambition."

"You... talk like he's in the past."

Simon nods. "He passed away, five years ago."

"I'm sorry to hear that."

"It's all right. I mean. I miss him, of course, for a lot of reasons, but I'm okay." He smiles. "I'm excited about your business; you'll have to model some clothes for me someday."

"Why do I get the feeling that if I did, there wouldn't be any clothes on me to model?"

"You get that feeling because you know me well." He grins and stands. "I'm glad you like the cookies."

"Thank you for making them. I'll walk you out."

I walk him to the foyer, which feels very formal. Not just because we're in this big fancy house but because after all we've done together, fighting and fucking, now I'm walking him to the front door like he was a traveling salesman I took pity on and let in for tea.

"Thank you," I tell him. "Seriously. You're the first person who's given me good advice instead of just telling me to give up and stop trying."

"Hey. I'll never tell you that. I might not have known you for long, but you're a woman who climbs a hedge to make sure her neighbor gets a piece of her mind." Simon grins at me. "Nothing's stopping you from getting what you want."

I feel a rush of warmth in my chest, and I get up onto my toes...

I plan to kiss him on the cheek. I swear. But somehow, he turns his head, or I miscalculate, and then, my mouth is moving against his.

We're kissing.

Chapter 8

Simon

Okay, I admit, when I showed up on Rose's doorstep I wasn't just hoping for a truce.

Her hanging up on me last night baffled me. I had no idea what'd happened. She sounded upset, almost, and I don't know what I did wrong. At least previously I knew why I'd upset her because I'd done it deliberately.

When I don't know how to work through a situation, I cook or bake. It helps clear my head. So I got up early this morning and I made some cookies. When I finished, I thought, hey, you know who might like these cookies?

Rose, that's who.

Nobody can resist my chocolate salted caramel cookies, especially when they're fresh out of the oven, so I walk over and tell her I want a truce. And I do mean it. I want us to stop fighting the way we have been. It gets my blood up, but I'd rather be fighting when we both know it's a prelude to fucking and not because we're actually genuinely upsetting each other.

Rose makes me feel alive, and damn it, I can't lose that. It's been too damn long. I need this. I need her.

I was hoping to just pick things up where they left off last night right away, but to my surprise, Rose seems almost shy. She's genuinely shocked to see me, that's for sure, and she leads me into the kitchen with this soft, bashful smile on her face that has my heart flipping in my chest.

From there we actually have a good conversation. I can't remember the last time I talked to someone about my dreams of being a chef. Most people look at it as some silly thing I wanted when I was younger, like when you're a kid and think you'll be an astronaut one day.

Most people look at my position and my success and they want that. They don't understand how it could be something I would trade in for another dream, if I could. But Rose seems to get it. She smiles as she listens to me, and she seems grateful for my advice. So grateful, in fact, that she kisses me as I'm leaving.

There's no way I can resist an invitation like that.

Rose's mouth presses to mine, and my whole body vibrates with heat. My hands fall to her hips and I yank her against me. Rose gasps against my mouth and I slide my tongue along the seam of her lips, then dart it inside of her mouth, teasing her.

She grabs onto my shoulders and rocks her hips into mine, and fuck, *yes*. This is what I was hoping for when I first showed up at her doorstep. Just hearing her voice over the phone wasn't enough. Hell, even if we'd been on a video call, it wouldn't have been enough. I need to touch her, to have her body against mine.

I need to be inside her.

We kiss frantically, pawing at each other's clothes. It's as good as the first time, maybe even more so, because while we're still frantic and passionate, we're not quite trying to punish each other. Fuck, I feel out of my mind as I get her shirt off, then her bra. I drop to my knees to get my mouth on her breasts as Rose gasps and shakes against me; then I remember what I said last night about returning the favor.

I get her onto the floor and yank down her jeans and her panties, exposing her to my gaze. I hitch her leg up over my shoulder and kiss along her thighs.

Rose moans, her fingers sliding desperately through my hair. "Simon... *Simon*..."

"Is this what you pictured last night?" I purr, nipping at the soft skin beneath my lips.

She moans. "Y-yes, yes, yes..."

I kiss further up until I'm right between her legs; then I dive in for the feast. I was a chef. I know how to appreciate a good meal. And Rose is a delicious one.

She's a determined, independent woman who doesn't let anything get in her way. How was I supposed to do anything except be attracted to her? I lick into her, sucking on her clit, unable to hold myself back enough to tease in spite of all my confident words last night.

I don't want to tease her and make her beg, at least not right now. I'm too keyed up myself for that. Instead, I make it my sole damn goal in life to make her orgasm as hard and as fast as possible, so hard and so fast that she's fucking dizzy with it.

Rose arches up into my mouth, tugging at my hair. "Simon, Simon, Simon," she chants, her voice music to my ears. Yeah, that's right, say my name.

I'm not generally a possessive type when it comes to women because I don't tend to date women. I just have fun with them and then we part ways amicably. But with Rose... yeah, I want her to scream my name and admit that I'm the one who's doing this to her. Hell, I want everyone in the damn neighborhood to hear us and know I'm the one making her feel this good.

It's probably the competitiveness. We started out fighting, and now I have her shaking on my tongue, against my lips. It feels like a hell of a victory, like fire in my blood.

"C'mon, baby." I slide two fingers into her and curl them. "I want to feel you. I want to *taste* you."

I dive back in, licking at her, and Rose screams out. She's shaking and clamping down on my fingers, desperate. "Simon—oh my God oh my fucking—"

She comes, and I lap it up, drunk on her orgasm. She's so fucking gorgeous, and my cock aches for her. I feel like I'm on fire.

I push up and undo my pants, pushing them down and kicking them off so we're skin on skin. She's so fucking warm and alive against me, arching and gasping, kissing me wildly like she wants to suck the taste of herself off my tongue.

"You want more, baby?" I ask in between frantic kisses. Her orgasm on my tongue doesn't seem to have sated her. If anything it seems to have made her even hungrier for me and more excited.

"Yes." Rose takes my face in her hands and looks me in the eye. "Fuck me, Simon."

Jeez, as if I'm going to say no to that. "You're insatiable."

It's a compliment, and judging by the smile Rose gives me as I kiss her again, I'm pretty sure she understands that. I stroke my cock, then guide it inside her, hitching one of her legs up over my hip. Fuck, she's so hot and tight. My mouth hangs open as I pant, my forehead pressing to Rose's. Rose wraps an arm around my shoulders, her fingers stroking the soft hair at the back of my neck. She's so feisty, but right now, she's soft and intimate.

It feels like victory. Like I earned that from her.

I push in, and in, and *in,* and then pull out, and then thrust in again. I feel that same overpowering animal instinct, that bone-deep connection I got when we fucked the first time. I start, and I don't stop. I keep going, thrusting into her, kissing her frantically until I can't anymore and my face falls into the crook of her neck, licking the sweat there, chasing the high we're both crashing into.

Rose claws at my back and shoulders, arching her hips up to meet my thrusts. I can feel the noises she makes against my lips as she moans and cries out my name.

"Yeah, that's it," I encourage her. She sounds so fucking good, yes, I want to hear her, I need to hear her… "C'mon, come for me, I know you can come again baby you're so fucking close, aren't you? You're so tight around me, I know you're close. You're ready to explode with it. You need it so badly, just give in. Make my cock even wetter, make me *feel* how good it feels for you, c'mon, sweetheart…."

Rose gasps, nails digging into my back as she shakes and orgasms. Holy fuck it feels so good. It feels so fucking good. I can't hold my climax back and I jerk, thrusting wildly as I come into her. We both slump down, me on top of Rose, and we breathe for a moment.

I almost want to laugh hysterically. We can't seem to stop doing this—fighting or keeping our hands off each other. But I'd like to try fixing it so that we're only doing one, not the other.

"Hey." I pull back, still breathing hard.

Rose looks up at me, smiling warmly. Her whole face is lit up. She's absolutely gorgeous, and my heart feels like it skips a beat. Look, I've been with a lot of women, but it was always casual. I never had time to date being a chef, then having to take over my father's company. It wasn't like I wanted more than a night anyway.

But Rose...

I hate my damn job. My close friend and the woman I rely on as my assistant is about to go on maternity leave. I'm going to have to deal with a new person, and I doubt it's going to be fun. Why shouldn't I take some time and focus on something other than work? Why not pursue what I feel with this woman? This connection that burns like a super-nova between us?

I kiss her and then pull away, sitting back on my knees. "We should clean up."

Rose laughs breathlessly. "Yeah, yeah, we should. Hold on."

She gets up and gets everything. I decide to wait until we're all put together again. I don't want her to think I'm only saying this because of the post-coital pleasure.

"Listen. I know we got off on the wrong foot. And then got off." I grin.

Rose snorts with laughter. "Uh-huh."

"But as shocking as it sounds, I like talking to you. I meant it, earlier, with the peace offering. I liked chatting with you. I was hoping we could do more chatting and try again properly this time, with me taking you out to dinner."

Rose's eyebrows rise, like that wasn't what she expected, even after everything. "You know you don't owe me dinner or anything, after all this."

"I know. I think you'd find a way to poison me for suggesting I do. I want to spend more time with you. And it would be nice to spend the time before sex eating some good food and chatting instead of climbing into each other's yards and arguing."

"You know, some people might find climbing a hedge romantic. Isn't that what Romeo did for Juliet?"

"They also ended up dead, so maybe we shouldn't follow their example."

Rose laughs. "All right."

"Yeah?"

I'll be honest, I was kind of expecting her to say no, just to spite me and to keep our chase going. Our "cat and mouse" has been a bit fun. I just want to move past it and see what else there is. I can't blame her if she wanted to keep the status quo.

But she doesn't. She said yes.

Relief floods my chest like cool water and I exhale. "Great. Friday at seven? I'll pick you up here?"

"I like it." Rose kisses me, her hands sliding up my chest.

I immediately start looking up restaurants when I get home. I'm going to blow her mind and finally get this relationship off to the right start.

Chapter 9

Rose

I feel like I'm floating on air.

I never would've expected this to happen. Not only did Simon and I have sex again, but he's asked me out on a date. I started out hating the guy. Then I felt ashamed of myself after the phone sex, wondering what I was getting myself into, confused about how I felt, and worried I was letting myself become some... plaything for a rich playboy.

I'm not going to just be the latest notch in someone's bedpost—someone he can booty call whenever he's just kinda feeling like it. Except, then he came over and offered me cookies, and we had a genuinely good talk. He gave me advice, he made me laugh, and I—I kissed him.

And holy fuck, he made me come like—like nobody ever has.

I don't want to say yes to a date just because the guy's good at eating me out. But I find myself saying yes because of the way that Simon smiles at me, and the way he looks at me, as he asks. Like maybe he's actually as nervous as I am, somewhere deep down. Like maybe he's softer than I gave him credit for being.

It can't hurt to go on just one date, right? At least that's what I tell myself. I find myself... excited. Looking forward to it.

Even anticipating it.

I don't see Simon for the rest of the week, but we text. Now that we're not fighting, I find that the banter is fun and lighthearted, and it keeps me distracted. He's funny. He's sharp, and he never backs down when he disagrees with me about something, whether it's my taste in music or a film that I liked and he didn't. It's invigorating to talk to someone who doesn't talk down to me when they disagree about something.

It feels like my whole life, my family disagreed with me in part because they didn't think I was capable of achieving my dreams. My "bad luck" was really just a symbol of the mistakes I was making in life. Simon just disagrees with me because he's a cranky, stubborn asshole who doesn't want to admit that maybe he could like a rom-com, and it's hilarious.

Nadia tells me that I'll finally meet Mr. Chaucer on Friday because I'll have my first official day working in the assistant position on Monday. Nadia's maternity leave will start, and I'll fully take over the role.

I'm more nervous about it than I thought I would be, so I'm glad I have this date to look forward to. Nadia's made it clear how Mr. Chaucer can be difficult to handle, but I figure he can't be worse than Simon. It's just that with Simon, I could snap back. Mr. Chaucer is my boss.

I suppose even if this goes terribly, I'll have my date to unwind on.

Everything with my training has gone well, though. Simon's asked me about my new job, but I've tried not to say anything to him, partially because I don't want to talk about it and partially because I don't want to tell tales out of school.

There's nothing really to talk about, anyway. It's an assistant job. I'm feeling pressure to get it all right because, well, this is the CEO of a massive company. But it's still just the stuff I had to do at my dad's office, and I don't really want to talk about it.

Luckily, Simon seems to understand. Probably because he doesn't want to talk about his job, either. All I know is that he took over the place from his own dad, and boy, can I relate to that. But he doesn't want to talk about it beyond that, he'd rather discuss other things like my plans for my fashion company or answer my questions about food and the restaurant business.

I'm more than happy to do that. We have to deal with our jobs forty hours a week, I'm not going to be the one who makes us talk about them the rest of the time.

Friday arrives and I'm equal parts excited and nervous. I have my date tonight. I find myself... well, what if we don't actually work when we're in a restaurant having a nice chat and not yelling at each other in Simon's front yard?

Nadia seems to think that whatever nerves she senses are about meeting my boss, which is fair. I am a bit nervous about that, too.

Focus on one thing at a time, I tell myself. No reason to worry about the date when I'm at work, at vice versa.

"He's anxious to meet you," Nadia tells me as she leads me to that distinctive office.

"Anxious, huh?"

Nadia smiles reassuringly. "I promise, he'll like you. I'm sure he'll appreciate your no-nonsense attitude."

I take a deep breath and smile back at her. Yeah, unless that attitude gets me fired.

Nadia knocks on the door. I've been in this office before while Nadia's trained me but it's always been empty.

"Come in."

I have a moment to think that voice sounds familiar before Nadia opens the door and steps in, bringing me with her. "Here she is, Mr. Chaucer. This is Rose. Rose, this is..."

My heart stops as I see a familiar figure stand up from behind his desk, his eyes wide with shock.

"Simon."

My boss is Simon.

Chapter 10

Simon

Holy fuck.

I gape in shock as Rose stands in front of me. Rose is my new assistant.

Nadia's been buttering me up about her, telling me all about how great my new assistant will be, how much I'll like her, and how quickly she's picking it all up. Personally, I've been skeptical. I trust Nadia's judgement but I'm unsure about this transition.

Now, I want to laugh hysterically, because Nadia's right. She's more right than she realizes. I do like my new assistant. I like her way too much.

"Everything okay?" Nadia looks back and forth between us.

There's no missing the shock on our faces, I'm sure. I don't know what my face looks like but I know that it's not anything normal, and Rose's eyes are huge and wide.

"Rose and I—we've met before." I think quickly. Nadia's loyal to me, but I know this office loves gossip. I can't let it get out that Rose and I have slept together. "At a—at a party. Through her cousin. Sorry, just—didn't expect that."

My heart feels like it's running a damn race as my mind spins out of control. Rose is my new assistant. Rose, the woman I've had sex with twice; that's not even counting the damn phone sex. Rose who I've been texting for days, excited by every conversation, looking forward to our date tonight.

Our date tonight.

Fuck.

I can't take her out, now. I had scoured the area trying to find the best place to take her, wanting to impress her without overwhelming her. I'm sure she's been to lots of fancy places before, given her cousin is my damn neighbor. Rose's family must have money. I hadn't wanted to just take her to the latest hot new place or some restaurant that just had a famous name attached. She won't be impressed by me throwing money around.

Instead, I had picked Geoffrey's, a gorgeous place in Malibu right on the water. The views are amazing, especially at sunset, and the food is delicious. I'm a fan of their paella, personally. I thought it would be a great romantic evening, and we could take a stroll on the beach afterward.

Nothing too crazy. No pulling out all the bells and whistles. But still something to show that I'm invested in this. Something that showed the thought I put into it.

I'm gonna have to call and cancel my reservation, I think, feeling a little hysterical.

I was worried about how today would go and reassured myself that even if I hated my new assistant, I would get to see Rose tonight. And now, I do like my new assistant, but I sure as hell won't be seeing Rose; she is my new assistant. I feel like I must've pissed off someone upstairs but good to have the universe laughing at me like this.

"Is this... going to be a problem?" Nadia asks.

She's really asking *did you piss this woman off? Did you hook up with her?* Nadia's been around me long enough that she knows I have a bit of a playboy reputation, but I have just as much of a reputation as an asshole who rubs people the wrong way.

Oh, don't worry, N, I've done both! I want to tell her. It's almost funny. Almost.

It's just that I really liked texting with Rose this week. I liked having someone to talk to about food and the restaurant business, someone who sounded like she really cared and listened. It was a lot of fun to banter with someone just for the sake of it, and not because I was pissing that person off or because I was actually angry.

Rose is funny. She doesn't back down. She's determined to live her life away from her family business. I can approve of that last part for sure. I wish I had the guts to do that. But Rose's parents are still alive, and I understand it's different. I just find myself wanting to give her what I couldn't give myself.

I've wondered what her family business is—maybe I know her father—but now she's here in front of me as my new assistant, and I'm confused. Her cousin is letting her stay at her place, but did the rest of her family cut her off? Is that why she has to work an assistant job?

"Not at all," I say, answering Nadia's question a beat too late.

Rose doesn't seem to be sure what to say at all. She's stopped gaping, but is now staring down at her hands like it might be dangerous to look anywhere else.

"I'd like to have a meeting with Rose to discuss her work with me," I continue. "Are you sure there's nothing else you need before you head out, N?"

"No, I'm good. The doctor put me on bed rest, but if

there's ever a question Rose has, I've told her to reach out to me. I might be lying down, but I can still talk; God knows I'll be bored out of my mind."

I worry for Nadia and her health, although I don't say it out loud. I know she'll rip me a new one for it. Nadia's tough, she's just also my friend, and, of course, I'll miss her. Even if right now I'll especially miss her because as long as she's gone, I can't have Rose in the way I really want.

"Great." I hug Nadia carefully, aware of her stomach. "Then do whatever you need to do, but you're free to go in my eyes. Rose, we'll discuss everything so you're ready to take over full-time from Nadia on Monday. Sound good?"

Rose nods. She smiles reassuringly at Nadia, who I don't think is fully convinced that everything's as fine as I claim. But Nadia says nothing more about it. She just hugs me back, tells me to take it easy on the new girl, and reminds Rose that she can use the stapler on my hand if I'm getting out of line.

I roll my eyes fondly and Rose smiles. I want to tell Nadia that oh, don't worry, Rose knows how to handle me when I get stubborn, but I can't, and it takes everything in me to keep my mouth shut as Nadia leaves, and it's just the two of us alone.

Just Rose and me. Rose, the woman I want to date, the woman who is now my immediate subordinate at work.

Fuck.

Chapter 11

Rose

When Nadia leaves, I'm simultaneously relieved and alarmed. I don't want her to stay any longer because I definitely can't lie well. I don't want her to find out about myself and Simon. But I also don't know what to do now that Simon and I are alone.

Simon clears his throat. "What are you doing taking an assistant job?"

I stare at him. "What kind of question is that?"

"Has your family cut you off that badly?"

"What the hell? No, they're not in California. I moved here."

"Can't you work for your cousin's company?"

I snort. "Yeah, right, I'm not doing that. I'm accepting enough charity staying at her place to housesit, thanks. I refuse to let my parents think I'm only surviving out here because our rich relatives took pity on me."

"So you're... not rich."

"Uh, did you think I was? I said the house wasn't mine!" My blood is boiling. "Are you angry because I'm not rich!?"

Simon blinks at me in confusion. "What? No, I'm just

fucking confused. You talked about your job and I thought it was something like—this."

He gestures around us at the office, presumably meaning something more like his own job as CEO.

"You talked about your family business and how you were getting a job, like what your father had trained you to do. You said that you didn't like it, but were just doing it while you launched your business."

"That's right." The gears in my head are turning. With Chloe being my cousin and Simon's own father being a CEO, I can see how he made the assumption that I was going to have a higher position than someone's assistant. "Is that a problem?"

"No, no, not at all." Simon shakes his head. "I just... I'm sorry, I'm upset, I'm confused, I don't know how this happened."

"A series of bad coincidences." I'm scouring my memory, trying to recall if Nadia ever said 'Simon' instead of 'Mr. Chaucer' in my presence. I feel a bit sick.

"Well, we're going to have to fix this."

"Oh, yeah, right, you're going to just shunt me off to some other department?" I snort.

"Well, what do you want me to do?" Simon retorts. "I thought I was going to get to take you on a date tonight, Rose, for fuck's sake. I don't care about your economic status. I care that now you're my goddamn assistant, and all I want to do is fuck you. You drive me crazy, and I can't handle it."

I swallow hard. Fuck, he's hot when he's angry. "It's not like I'm happy about it," I snap. "You think I'm any less upset about it than you are?"

Simon walks around me to the door, making sure it's locked. As he passes me our shoulders brush, and I shiver with heat. The last few times I've seen this man, we ended up having sex. It's hard to convince my body that's not what's happening right now, or about to happen.

Simon turns back to me, his eyes dark as he drags his gaze over my body. I can feel myself flushing.

"It's not my fault this happened," I point out. "If you'd actually been into work at any point during this time, I would've known it was you, and we would've worked this out ages ago."

"And maybe if you'd told me more about your job," Simon snaps, walking up to me. "I would've realized where you worked and this wouldn't have happened."

"So you wouldn't have slept with me?" I point out.

"Well," Simon smirks. "Maybe."

I snort, poking him in the chest. "Face it. We're in this mess because you couldn't do your damn job. I fail to see how that's my fault."

"It's your fault for being fucking irresistible," Simon grumbles, as if to himself; he's so grumpy and annoyed, not at me, but at the entire situation. I find myself laughing.

Because yeah, the situation sucks. And if Simon didn't drive me so crazy, this would be a lot easier. I could agree and say that we could've done one thing or another differently, but really, would either of us have believed that a coincidence was possible? You don't look for what you don't expect to see.

"Glad to know you find me irresistible," I tease him.

Simon looks at me, as if he sees right through my teasing. It gives me reassurance to know that I'm not just a notch on a bedpost. His hands land on my hips and he tugs me in against him.

"Trust me, you are annoying in how much I want to put my hands on you."

"You're putting your hands on me right now." I grab his shirt and tug him in.

I don't mean to kiss him, I don't even know what I'm thinking, but Simon leans in and it turns into a kiss, hungry and demanding. I kiss him back, wanting him, angry at the situation and once again channeling it into lust. It's like we can't help ourselves.

"I kept thinking about what I'd do to you tonight," Simon murmurs, his hands all over me.

I laugh, feeling a little hysterical. "I kept thinking—even if I hated my boss—I would get to see you tonight—and you could fuck out my frustration—make me forget—"

Simon chuckles, clearly feeling the same way, angry and laughing at the strange humor at the same time. He pushes me back until my ass hits his desk and I push up onto it, spreading my legs. I'm glad I decided to wear a cute skirt and blouse today. I had put it on because I wasn't sure if I'd have time to go home and change before my date tonight, and I'd wanted to be ready.

"I dressed like this for you," I admit in a whisper between frantic kisses. "I couldn't wait for you to see me later on our date..."

"Are these clothes you designed?" Simon asks. I can feel heat shudder through me like it never has before.

Nobody's asked me that. Nobody's ever asked me, hey, are you wearing clothes that you designed?

"Yes," I admit. "I sewed these myself."

"Then it would probably be bad form if I ripped them off you," Simon murmurs.

Fuck, that's hot. "If you don't mind."

I'm sure he can hear the smile in my tone, but he doesn't try and rip my clothes. He just pushes my skirt up and my panties down.

"I wish I could get you naked," Simon admits, even as he grinds against me. Fuck, I can feel how hard he is, the hot throb of his cock answering the desperate throb between my legs.

"Later," I blurt out, even though I know there probably won't be a later.

Hell, there shouldn't even be a now, but I'm too busy undoing his pants. I wrap my hand around his cock, stroking it, feeling the heat of it as I draw him to me. He's so thick, and all I want is to have him inside me again, to feel him stretching me. I whimper as he slowly thrusts inside of me. Then Simon's kissing me harshly to keep me quiet as he thrusts into me.

All of the nerves I was feeling about today, between meeting my boss and going on this date, have spun around and turned into this sex—all of the energy transferred into kissing Simon, taking him inside of me, clenching around him, and digging my heels into his back.

When I'd thought about the sex I'd hoped to have tonight, I'd pictured actually being in a bed this time. I'd pictured us having hours, taking our time, getting to really explore one another.

This isn't anything like that, this is the tidal wave of emotion taking us over once again.

I'd find more time for regret if I wasn't busy getting fucked so hard and so well. Simon stays deep inside of me, fucking me with short little thrusts that don't rock the sturdy desk, keeping us quiet in case anyone walks by. It's so hot, the idea that someone could catch us, even though it's so, so wrong. I whimper into his mouth as he tugs at my hair and keeps my head in place to kiss me.

I've never had sex like this, where we could so easily be caught, and it's exhilarating, adding to the adrenaline in my body. I feel like I'm on a rollercoaster, the big drop approaching, and I can't wait for us to get there. Simon speeds up, his breath hot against my neck as he pants and growls. I claw at him, trying to get him even deeper, clenching down around him, spiraling higher and higher as that drop comes—

I gasp, swallowing my moan just in time as I come with a shudder, and Simon groans into my neck and jerks and spills into me. Fuck, fuck, that's so hot, we're fucking on his desk at work; it shouldn't be hot but it is, it really, really is. The forbidden nature of it just makes it so sexy.

We pant together, Simon jerking a bit into me, like he's trying even now to fuck his spend even deeper inside of me. There's something so possessive about it that makes me shiver, like he's not even trying to be, he just can't help himself. Then he goes stiff, and before I can even register the change, he's ripping himself away from me and staring at me in horror.

"Fuck." Simon runs a hand through his hair, then grimaces. "That was a mistake. We shouldn't have done this, that was a terrible mistake."

My heart falls into my stomach, because as much as I hate to hear it...

He's right.

Chapter 12

Simon

I have to find a way to get some damn self-control around this woman.

I was looking forward to seeing Rose tonight. I wanted to see her so fucking badly. I was planning to take her home and spend all damn night worshipping that tight ass and her gorgeous breasts, every dip and curve of her body, and making her scream my name.

Even though she's now my employee, it's like I can't fully turn that off. Now, I'm fucking her on my damn desk.

She's so sexy, and I have to admit, doing this on my desk where anyone could come knocking on my door at any second makes it even sexier. Rose makes these tiny adorable noises, these gasps and swallowed moans as she struggles to stay quiet, and I fucking love it. I love the forbidden nature of it. I love how forcing ourselves to be quiet makes every other aspect of the sex that much stronger. I love how fucking deep I am inside her—

But we can't keep doing this. She's my employee.

Even though our relationship started before there was any power dynamic, now I have the power to fire her. This is a PR nightmare waiting to happen. HR would have a field day if they found out and that's even without the fucking we just had in my damn office.

My *office*. God this woman drives me insane like nobody else.

I never would've even thought of doing something like this in my office with a woman, never mind an *employee*. Fuck. I pull away from Rose as if she's burned me; I hurry to find the tissues that are somewhere in one of my desk drawers. I feel half-insane, like when I was a teenager and desperately getting off in my room and terrified my mom of all people would find out, and how embarrassing that would be.

Rose cleans herself up as well. She doesn't look happy about this, either, which is comforting in a weird way. She's not seeing this as nonchalant or no big deal.

"What are we going to do?" she whispers.

I brace my hands on the desk and let my head fall forward. "We're not doing that again, that's for sure."

"I liked it," she admits in a rush. "I know—we won't do it again, I'm not saying we should, you're my boss, but. It was hot."

"Yeah. It really, really was." I look up at her and I see the pleased smile on her face. I smirk back at her before the smile on my face drops away. I push myself up to stand up straight.

"I need this job," Rose blurts out. "If I have any hope of having spare money to start my company—I need this. My cousin will be gone for a bit so I figure I can start things, get the ball rolling you know, while I don't have to pay rent or anything. She's even letting me borrow one of her fancy BMWs to drive so I don't need a car. I can put everything into my company. And then when she gets back..."

"You hope it'll be up and running and making you money."

Rose nods.

"And if you can't do the company full time once she gets back..." I groan, knowing the answer.

"Then I'd still need a job like this in the meantime to pay my rent." Rose winces. "I love my cousin but she's, uh. She's not easy to live with. I don't think she'd want me to stick around."

"Her house is huge!"

"You'd be surprised," Rose says dryly.

I run my hand through my hair and then wince again. People are going to wonder why my hair's all over the place now.

Rose walks up to me and begins fixing my hair, probably guessing why I winced. "I need this job," she murmurs.

"I know. I'm not going to fire you just so I can date you."

"I wish you could," Rose admits. "Can you move me to another department?"

"That'll just look suspicious. People will want to know why I did that an hour after meeting you. And I can't leave this position open. I don't know what details N gave you, but her doctor ordered her on bed rest for the remainder of her pregnancy. She wanted to keep working right up until around her due date, but her body's just taking the whole thing hard."

"She... she said something about needing to rest a lot, yes." Rose grimaces. "You call her N."

"Yeah. Nadia's my friend, that's my nickname for her."

"Well. When you mentioned work, and you mentioned N..."

Oh, God. Another way we didn't know that I was going to be her boss. Rose never mentioned Nadia by name, and I called Nadia by her nickname, so neither of us could put two and two together. I groan. "This is just such a mess."

"Could I train someone else to take my place?"

"If you can come up with a good reason why you're transferring departments, or why another department should even hire you. People talk in this office, Rose, they'll immediately know something's up, and I'm not going to fire you."

"So we're stuck."

I nod. Rose looks miserable. I don't feel all that much better about it, but I know it's what we have to do. We have to act like nothing happened, and we have to stay apart. We can't date. Not if we're going to avoid becoming a scandal.

My father would roll over in his grave if I let anything damage his beloved company. I can't let anything happen to it. I can't do anything that will damage Rose's reputation, either. She just got this job and was trained; if people found out and she had to quit and look for somewhere else, or even worse was fired...

I'd give her a glowing recommendation, of course I would, but would that really take the sting out of it? We have no choice but to abandon our personal relationship and keep this professional relationship up until there's another solution.

I can't ask her to go looking for another job right away. I guess I'll just have to hope that her company does in fact take off and she's able to make a profit out of it so that she can quit. In the meantime, this is going to be torture.

"This won't be permanent," I promise her, even though I don't know how it's going to go or how long. "We just have to keep our hands to ourselves and act professional until you don't need this job anymore."

Rose nods. "No pressure." Her voice is weak.

"Hey, no, no pressure." I take her hands. "Listen to me. I'm not going to ask you to rush getting your company launched just so we can have sex or even try dating. You do whatever you need to do at the pace you need to do it at, okay?"

Rose nods, but then rolls her eyes and says, "Don't get all soft on me, now, *Mr. Chaucer*. Your assistant's been warning me all week about how cranky you can get. I know firsthand how much you like to argue."

"I'll do my best." I mean it. I can't be seen treating Rose differently from any other employee. "We can do this. It'll be fine."

I can have some self-control around this woman. I've never been unable to control myself or been unable to resist temptation before, there's no reason for me to fail now. Except that it's so much harder than I ever expected.

Rose is excellent at her job. I'm sure that the people who have to deal with me don't appreciate it, but she has no time to suffer fools; she's matter-of-fact and no-nonsense. I love letting her deal with annoying people before I do.

Most people are used to Nadia, who didn't like to suffer fools either, but had a gentler approach. It's clear that Rose doesn't care about making friends here, though. She has no problem pointing out when people are wasting my time or talking in a way that isn't professional.

Some of the other C-level executives try to complain to me about her, stating they've never been spoken to like this before—how could she, and all that jazz. I just grin and tell them that maybe they need to shape up their behavior.

Having Rose as my pit bull at the door gets rid of all of the bullshit I have to deal with; damn it, I find myself enjoying coming into work. Not as much as I'd like coming into work if I owned a restaurant, but it's fun to watch her deal with people and it cuts down on the shit I have to work through. Of course, I'm not spared, either.

I hate working here, and it's hard for me to hide that all the time. Rose has no problem setting me straight. We often end up arguing, trying to keep our voices down while my office door is open.

The open door is a policy I've implemented; and so far, Rose hasn't tried to close it. She knows why it's there even though I haven't told her why I always keep it open. Keeping it closed would just be far too big a temptation, for the both of us. Or at least for me.

Rose insists on calling me by my last name, which is professional; but every time she narrows her eyes and snaps in a low voice, trying not to let anyone overhear, "*Mr. Chaucer*," and then proceeds to chew me out about something, I want to grab her and bend her over my desk before she can even finish her sentence.

Only that open door keeps me from doing something stupid. What makes it worse is that I'm not the only one who's noticed how damn hot Rose is when she's angry.

I don't think she's realized it, somehow, because she hasn't shut anyone down the way I know she's capable of doing; but she isn't flirting with anyone, either. But the men in the office love to find stupid excuses to stop by her desk and chat, asking her how she's doing and to please ask them for any help... would she like a coffee from the break room...

It's infuriating because I can't do anything about it, not really. I can't claim Rose. She's not mine to claim, not as long as she's my assistant. Sometimes, I wonder if I did something bad in a past life and this is my punishment.

"Did you have your lunch break yet?" one of the guys from the marketing department asks, leaning on Rose's desk. "There's this fantastic Greek place down the street..."

I get up from my desk and walk over to the doorway. "Lerner, aren't you supposed to be on the other side of the building?"

Lerner startles. "Uh. Mr. Chaucer, sir. I didn't see—I didn't realize you were at your desk."

"I like to be full of surprises that way." I smile and try not to make it an obvious smirk. "Lerner, are you bothering my assistant when she's trying to get her work done?"

"No, sir, I was just…"

"Because I've noticed her struggling to get her work completed with people like you interrupting her all day. All of you are out of your actual departments—where you should be doing actual work—so you can come and bother my assistant. I don't recall having a meeting with any of you, so there should be no reason for you to stop here, right?"

"…right." Lerner deflates.

"That's what I thought. We're here to work, Lerner, not bother our women coworkers. You might want to remind your fellow workers of that."

I go back into my office, leaving the door pointedly open once again, and sitting back down at my desk. Lerner mutters something to Rose and then hurries away. Rose types at her computer for a moment, then picks up the phone and dials.

My desk phone rings. I pick it up. "Hello, Simon Chaucer speaking."

"You really didn't have to do that," Rose says quietly into the phone.

"The guys are all flirting with you, it's bullshit."

"And you just had to pee in a circle around me, huh?" She sounds amused, luckily, rather than upset.

"You're my assistant, and I don't appreciate you being

distracted by a bunch of men who don't know how to flirt if their lives depended on it."

"Of course, it's just that I'm your assistant. That's all it is."

I level a glare at the back of her head, one that she can't see. I'm sure that she can tell, though, just like I'm sure she's smirking at the phone right now even though I can't see it.

"Whatever else is going on," I say, lowering my voice to a rumble, "you are my assistant, and I don't appreciate you being interrupted. I don't want you distracted while you're trying to do your job because if you're distracted, then my schedule can get fucked up."

"That's fair. I wasn't encouraging them, just for the record."

"I didn't think you were."

"Oh. Good. I just didn't see a need to cause problems by shooing them away."

I know what she means. "Well, now you can just say that I'll get angry if I catch them talking to you."

"I appreciate it, boss, thank you."

"You're welcome. I'm truly an amazing boss that way."

"Of course you are."

"Are you placating me?"

"I would never," Rose scoffs, and then she hangs up.

I grin as I hang up the phone, but I still feel an annoyance stirring in my chest. These men aren't going to be deterred completely by their boss telling them to lay off his secretary. They're just going to be sneakier about it. And I can't do a damn thing. If I get too possessive of Rose when I didn't care about Nadia, people are going to talk.

This is definitely torture. I have no idea how I'm supposed to survive this.

Chapter 13

Rose

I have to admit that Simon's anger over some of the men flirting with me is funny, but that's the only funny thing about this entire situation. I can't afford to quit this job, but working with Simon when I can't have him is torture.

We argue. Of course we do. Nadia wasn't lying when she said Simon's stubborn.

"You have to at least put in an appearance at this meeting," is something I say so many times that I think I'm going to start muttering it in my sleep.

Simon's good at his job, damn good, but he has very little patience for the idiots he has to deal with. I can't blame him but that means that *I'm* the one who has to deal with them instead.

At least he seems to enjoy it when I tear people a new one. I've never had a boss that just let me loose like that before. I know it's because dealing with me is still, at the end of the day, easier than dealing with Simon. But I like it.

It's easy for me to be the dog guarding the gate when I peer into his office and see him with his elbows on the desk, his head in his hands. I think everyone else just sees Simon as some kind of hardass; but really, he's miserable here. It's so easy for me to see that I wonder how other people are missing it, but I think it's just that people see what they want to see.

Simon's the CEO of a powerful company. Who wouldn't want that position? Who wouldn't want that power and privilege and money? Everyone else here likes their jobs, or at least seems to like them well enough to appreciate the benefits they give. I don't think it occurs to them to want something else.

I pause by Simon's open door in the evening before I leave, leaning against the doorframe. He always keeps the door open, no matter what. I get the feeling he never did that with Nadia.

"It's clear he doesn't trust you," one of the other assistants told me in the break room, rolling her eyes. "It's so obvious. He depended completely upon Nadia, and I don't think he believes anyone else could do as good of a job."

"He's a good boss to me," I told her. I left the break room because I wasn't going to gossip about my boss.

I'm not interested in all of that. Even if Simon was a shitty boss, and he's not, I wouldn't gossip about it. That kind of stuff always comes back to bite you in the ass in some way. No, thank you. Besides, I know the real reason he keeps the door open. He's never said it, but I know if the door was closed, I'd want to give into temptation. And I know he feels the same; it would be too dangerous.

Now, as I lean against the door frame, I don't see someone who's cranky or wants to fight. I just see someone who's tired.

"You doing okay?" I murmur. "Boss?"

Simon looks up, snorting with amusement when I tack

on the word at the end. "I'm fine." He groans and rolls his shoulders.

I want to walk over and put my hands on him, massage his shoulders and the back of his neck, but that would be inappropriate. I hate this. I hate how I want him and I can't have him.

Just when we were about to explore our relationship outside of our arguments, just as we were about to get deeper with each other, the arguing and banter is all we're allowed to have.

"You're not fine," I point out quietly. I dare to step further into the office, just so nobody can easily overhear us, but I keep the door open. "Look, I'm happy to take on anyone in this company who only cares about profit or can't do their jobs properly, but I don't like that you're miserable."

Simon shrugs, turning off his computer and standing up. He takes off his jacket and tie and rolls up the sleeves of his blue button-up shirt where I can see his forearms. Fuck, he's hot. I want him to pick me up and pin me against the wall. "This company meant everything to my father. I want to make sure his legacy is taken care of; he'd be disappointed if I wasn't looking after it."

I fold my arms. "So you're supposed to spend your life unhappy to appease someone who's already gone? I don't think a genuinely good parent would want that for you."

Simon snorts. "Right, because your parents are so supportive."

I glare at him, and he softens. "Sorry. I shouldn't have said that."

"No, you're right." I sigh. "My parents love me, but they don't actually support my choices. I don't think they're bad parents but..."

"It's complicated." Simon gathers his things. "I'll see you tomorrow?"

"You will."

Simon's hand brushes against mine as he walks past me, slowly, and my breath hitches. I can see his throat bob as he swallows. "Have a good night, Rose."

I want to beg him to come over. I want to text him and joke about climbing over the hedge. We're next-door neighbors, for crying out loud, we could see each other at home, and nobody here would ever have to know.

But I know how that goes. It's hard enough already when we're not sleeping together. How much more difficult would it get if we actually do, even if we keep it to our off hours?

I let him leave, and I go to clean up my desk.

"Hey, Rose?"

I look up. It's one of the other assistants, the one I was talking to the other day who said Simon was a crappy boss who didn't trust me. I struggle to remember her name. "Hey, Michelle."

Michelle smiles tentatively. "Look, I just wanted to let you know, uh, I know it's probably not my place, but I really wouldn't... just a word of advice, y'know, don't shit where you eat."

I blink at her. "What do you mean?"

Did she hear Simon and me just now? Does she suspect that there's something between us?

Michelle shakes her head. "It's okay, you don't have to lie to me. I know that some people are judging you for it, but I'm just worried. I know it's tempting, and you think it's all just fun and games, but you can't put your job on the line for something like this. It's never worth it."

"Michelle, you're going to have to tell me what you

84

mean because I'm genuinely confused. What are people saying? What are they judging me for?"

I manage to keep my tone calm, but my heart hammers in my chest. I just pray nothing shows on my face.

Michelle frowns. "The... uh. I don't know how to say it without..." She clears her throat. "David was talking about it. How you slept with him and also whatshisname in marketing? And the IT guy?"

I stare at her, all nerves about Simon draining away to be replaced by true confusion. "What the fuck? What do you—David? From the *graphics* department?"

"Yeah, him."

"He asked me out to lunch a few days ago. I said no. Lerner from PR tried the same thing and Simon chewed him a new one. I don't even know what IT guy you mean. I don't know if I've spoken to an IT person face to face this whole time, I've just emailed them."

Michelle shakes her head. "Look, you don't have to—"

"I didn't sleep with anyone!" I snap. "What the actual fuck? Do I look like I want to lose my job? Just sleeping with one person is an HR nightmare waiting to happen; why would I sleep with a bunch of people? Those dogs have been asking me out since day one, and I've said no. I guess David couldn't handle that. I'm not shitting where I'm eating or whatever you want to call it."

Michelle's eyes go wide and she takes a small step back, unable to handle my anger. "Okay, I'm sorry. I shouldn't have assumed."

"Damn right, you shouldn't have. David's a piece of shit. I keep to myself at work. Full stop." I gather my things and march past her. "Have a great night, I guess."

As much as I put on an air of bravado in front of Michelle, my stomach clenches in fear. I feel sick all night, and I almost want to call in sick to work. I can't do that, though. I can't show fear. I can't let David or anyone else know I'm upset. I have to act like nothing is wrong.

I come into the office and immediately Simon calls me in. "Rose!"

"Yes, my liege?" I enter the office and find him tearing his desk apart.

"Where the fuck is the contract for the Maui resort?"

"It's in the folder on my desk, where I told you it would be, because it needed the copyedit revisions, remember?"

Simon groans. "I need to review it, there's apparently a counter-offer."

"Oh no, a counter-offer for a prime resort in one of the most popular vacation spots in the world. Who could have foreseen this?"

"I don't need your sarcasm today, Rose, seriously." Simon storms past me and grabs the folder from my desk, before storming back. "Would it fucking kill you to just be nice to me sometimes? Or nice to anyone?"

"Oh, yeah, I bet you want me to be nice to everyone. Do you want me to start being nice to all the men asking me out? You'd sure love that."

"Don't act like you liked it, either, you would've turned them down even if I hadn't intervened."

"Well, maybe you should've intervened more," I snap before I can stop myself.

Simon pauses, dropping the file on his desk. "What do you mean?"

"Nothing. It's nothing. Just read your stupid contract and don't complain to me if there are typos."

I turn away, but Simon says, "Your hands are shaking."

"I'm just angry at you." I try to walk out of the office, but I feel Simon hurrying up behind me.

"Rose, I know you, you don't let me get to you. Unless I did, and I'm sorry, what's wrong?"

"*Nothing.*" Even as I say it, I can feel my voice crack; the next thing I know, tears are slipping free.

Simon stares at me in shock, and then he breaks the rule. He goes and closes the office door.

Chapter 14

Simon

Rose is *crying*.

I'm shocked. Rose doesn't strike me as someone who cries easily. Someone comes at her, she snaps right back at them. God knows she's had no problem coming at me when I've been cranky and short-tempered.

"What's wrong? Is it me?" If I've done something wrong to truly upset her, I'll change it.

Rose is a firecracker, and it's clear to me that she's had to be. If her family didn't support her and she had to come out to Los Angeles all alone, she's had no choice but to believe in herself. What else could she do? No one else believed in her.

Someone got to her, and if I was that person, I'll never forgive myself. "Did I take things too far?"

Rose shakes her head. Since I closed the door she's crying harder, like she feels safe to do it now that people can't walk by and see. "It's not you."

"Okay, okay, c'mere." I pull her into a tight hug and kiss

the top of her head. "It's okay. You're okay." I rub her back. "Tell me what it is."

"It's stupid, honestly, it doesn't matter." Rose pulls away and wipes her eyes, trying to do it so she doesn't get her face red and people don't realize she's cried.

"If it made you cry, then it matters."

Rose sighs. "You know how Lerner was trying to ask me out? And how he wasn't the only one?"

"Did he do something?"

"Someone else did. David. He works in another department. But he did mention Lerner. He was telling people that I've been sleeping around with different people."

The blood in my veins boils. "*What.*"

I am going to commit a damn murder if I have to. "They're claiming you—what the *fuck*."

Rose pats her eyes. I go to my desk and get tissues, handing them to her. "I'll handle this."

"You don't have to—Simon—"

"No. Listen." I turn back to her and grab her gently by the shoulders. "Even if I didn't want to date you—even if there was nothing between us—nobody at my company gets to say that shit about you. We treat people well here and if some guy can't handle being rejected, then that's his problem. It sure as fuck isn't yours. As your boss, it's my job to deal with this."

I pull away and yank open the door, then head over to David's department. I know who she's talking about since I saw him hanging around her desk a few days ago. I didn't think anything of it other than, of course, annoyance that some asshole who didn't even deserve her was flirting. I can't have her, but now I'm fucking steamed.

David's at his desk chatting with one of the other guys as they look at the computer screen. He could be doing work or he could be showing the other guy a picture of a cat for all I know. "David."

He looks up and the other guy's eyes go wide. Eric? Is that his name? "Mr. Chaucer, sir."

"Yeah, you'd better 'sir' me. I hope you remember to talk to your new boss that way too because you're about to be out of a fucking job."

Everyone's staring now.

David looks completely confused. "Sir?"

"I just asked my assistant to get me a file and she burst into tears. Want to know why? Because she just learned that you're spreading a rumor about her sleeping around with a bunch of her coworkers. Including you."

David goes white as a sheet. Somewhere to the side, I hear someone drop a pen in shock, the sound of it clattering on the hardwood of the office floor.

"How do you know she's telling the truth?" David splutters. "She's making that shit up, I never said anything."

"Right, because the one thing we've all noticed about Rose in her couple of weeks working here is how she cries at everything, is afraid of confrontation, and will talk behind people's backs," I point out. "You and I both know that you wanted to date her and she turned you down. She's turned everyone down. I've had to sit there in my office and deal with you idiots bothering her while she should be working.

"If you're the kind of man who can't handle rejection and has to spread vile rumors to make yourself feel better, then you're not the kind of man I want working in my company. So we're going to HR, and we're getting you fired, right the fuck now. Start packing your things."

David just gapes at me, apparently in shock. Everyone else seems to be in shock, too.

Eric coughs. "Um, sir. Isn't this... kind of hearsay?"

"Oh? So is there anyone here who would like to deny that they heard a rumor about Rose sleeping around? Or that David was the one who spread the rumor? Raise your hands! Raise 'em high! I mean it. Because if Rose is the one lying, then I need to know and fire her."

Nobody raises a hand.

One woman, a tiny brunette with frizzy hair, speaks up. Her voice is like a mouse, but that's probably because I'm a raging bull right now and she's scared. "I was the one who told Rose about it, last night. I thought she really was, um, doing those things. I warned her that it's not a smart idea to uh. Do that. Where you work."

"I agree, personally. If you want to sleep around then have fun, but we have company policies for a reason. I highly recommend you not sleep around with your coworkers. But, if you do, that doesn't make you less of a person. My anger is not if Rose did or didn't sleep around, my anger is that this scumbag *lied* that she slept with him *and others* because he can't fuckin' handle that she doesn't want his second-rate dick. Am I clear?"

Everyone nods vigorously.

"We don't ruin people's lives with that kind of bullshit around here. I won't tolerate it. We treat the women in this company with *respect*. If she doesn't want to go out with you, she doesn't fuckin' want to go out with you. Am I clear?"

Again, everyone nods.

"Good." I look over at David, who still hasn't moved. "Get your ass in gear, I told you to pack it up."

I watch him pack, then drag his sorry ass to HR so we can get everything sorted. I don't want him suing me down the line, so we're going to do all of this properly. Rose has to make a statement, and so does the woman who piped up. A few others come forward, mostly women, but also a few men who seem eager to get into my good graces by showing what standup sorts they are.

Yeah, gimme a fuckin' break. I have no doubts that they spread and encouraged those rumors, but I can't prove anything. I just hope that in making an example out of David and humiliating him in front of the others, I've made it clear this kind of thing won't be tolerated.

Once it's all settled and I get back to my office, I find Rose at her desk. She's just staring at the computer, clearly not seeing anything on the screen even with her hands on the keyboard, frozen.

"Hey." I gently put my hand on her shoulder. "You okay?"

She shakes me off. "I'm okay. Thank you."

"It's been a long day." I look at the clock. Four p.m. "Would you like me to drive you home?"

Rose looks down at her hands, then exhales slowly and nods. "Yeah, that'd be really nice."

I nod. "Let me get my things."

She deserves a damn break after today, and I need to be more aware of what's going on with my employees. I won't ever let something like that happen again to someone who works for me, especially not Rose.

I might not be able to have her, but I can protect her, and I always will.

Chapter 15

Rose

I don't know what to expect when I admit the truth to Simon. I didn't want to tell him. I didn't want this to be a big deal. I didn't want David and anyone else spreading this rumor here to think that they affected me or upset me. Never let them see your belly, that's my motto.

But when Simon was being cranky I guess... he wasn't even being that bad, not really, but somewhere along the way, he became a safe place for me. So when he asks, I find myself falling apart before I even realize that's what's happening.

I don't expect anything to come out of it. I'm embarrassed for even letting it get to me, and I assume Simon will tell me to buck up and ignore it. It's just a stupid rumor and anyone who's been paying attention saw me shoot those men down and knows that it didn't happen.

Instead, Simon defends me. He chews David out publicly and drags him to HR and fires him.

I can't believe it.

Nobody's ever stuck up for me like this in my entire life. I can already hear my family's voices in my head telling me that if I'd been nicer, if I'd handled the situation better, then this wouldn't have happened. Or they would've sighed and said *you really do have the worst luck* the way they always do.

Maybe I'm not giving them enough credit. This is a pretty damn serious accusation that David was making about me, after all. I don't think Dad would've stood for someone talking about his daughter like that at his office. But it would've been because I was his daughter, and I still think I would've gotten some teasing for it at home. I'm too abrasive, I don't make the right choices...

Not Simon, though. Simon stood up for me. Simon humiliated this man in front of everyone *for me*. It makes my head spin. Simon lets me leave early since I do still feel, even with his defense, like I'm in a fishbowl. As we walk to the car he says quietly, "If you need to take a day or two off, you can work from home. I'll be fine at the office."

"No, you won't," I say just as quietly. "You'll kill someone before lunch."

Simon snorts with laughter and we reach his car, getting in. "I can behave myself!"

"Sure you can."

I watch Simon start up the car and pull out of the parking garage, driving out onto the street. "You really didn't have to do that."

"Of course I did. Any decent boss would make sure that was handled immediately. It's a form of sexual harassment."

"Most people would've just gone quietly to HR and had me file a report, let the department handle it."

"Well. I'm not most people."

"You really stood up for me. Thank you."

Simon glances at me as he drives. "You sound surprised.

You deserve for people to stand up for you like that. Not quietly. Loudly. No questions asked."

I shrug.

Simon keeps one hand on the wheel but reaches over with the other and takes my hand, squeezing. "Look." His eyes are on the road but I have no doubt that his attention is on me. "I know that you're used to your family finding a way to criticize everything you do. But you deserve better. You should expect better from people in your life."

I squeeze his hand back and he lets go, putting both hands on the wheel again. "Thank you."

It's hard to believe I started out hating this man. Simon's stubborn and doesn't like to be told what to do—like stop doing construction on his home early in the morning—but he's a good person. He looks out for women, and for me, in a way that I'm just not used to from men. How am I supposed to handle not getting to be with him when he keeps doing things like this?

"It's just—I probably could have done things differently," I point out. "I'm sorry if I made anything worse."

"Why are you apologizing?"

"Well I think it's pretty clear I pissed people off."

"And? That's their problem." Simon pulls into the driveway of Chloe's house, stops the car, and looks over at me. "Rose, I love how strong-willed and intelligent you are. You're a fantastic assistant, and I know you'll be a fantastic business owner. Those men shouldn't have been so aggressive about trying to ask you out in the first place. If they're attracted to you because of your attitude, they can't then get mad when that attitude is turned on them. You did nothing wrong."

My eyes blur and I wipe at them. I want him so badly. I want to be comforted, and he makes me feel safe, and I don't know how else to express how I'm feeling. I lean over and kiss him.

Simon goes stiff with shock for a moment, but then he's pushing into me, kissing me fiercely, his tongue sliding over my lips. I part them and he slides inside like he owns me, and maybe he does, his tongue stroking mine and adding kindling to the fire that starts in my stomach.

I grab his shoulders, trying to haul him closer and crawl into his lap at the same time, and Simon grunts, undoing our seatbelts and yanking me across the gear shift into his lap. I spread my legs, grinding down, gasping as he thrusts his hips up into me and I can feel him growing hard against me.

"Fuck, yes." Simon starts to slide his hands down from my face to my shoulders, further down, to my breasts. I arch up, exposing my neck to his greedy mouth, wanting him...

Simon yanks himself back and grabs the door handle, shoving the door open. "You need to get out."

His voice is rough, but not angry, and I realize what he means. I scramble out, putting distance between us. The two of us breathe heavily, struggling to get our breaths back.

"I'm sorry." Simon grips the steering wheel with one hand and I see that his knuckles are white with trying to get a grip. "We—we can't. Fuck."

"I know, I know. I shouldn't have—I'm sorry."

We both avoid looking at each other. I want him so fucking badly, but we can't do this. If we do it at home, if we tell ourselves it's okay, and we can make it work, we'll just be paving our road to hell with good intentions. It'll bleed over into work, and if it was ever found out, I wouldn't just be out of a job. Simon would be in massive trouble.

Hell, the standing up for me he just did would look bad. It would look less like he stood up for an employee the way he should for anyone—more like he was staking a claim, marking his territory. David could possibly sue.

We have to keep it platonic.

Simon takes a deep breath and exhales slowly. "You're okay?"

I nod. "Thank you for driving me home."

"Of course." Simon inhales, looking like he might say something more, but then he shakes his head a little and says, "Goodnight, Rose."

"Goodnight, Simon."

He closes the car door. I watch him pull out of the driveway and head to his house, just next door to me, so close and yet so far away. I go into the house and collapse on the couch in the living room, staring up at the ceiling. On the one hand, I feel comforted, knowing Simon has my back and this whole... *issue* at work has been cleared up. On the other hand, I'm sad because the one person I want is the one person I can't have. And I don't know what to do.

Chapter 16

Simon

The next couple of weeks are... subdued. Tense, even.

Rose is quiet and so am I. The entire office is a bit subdued, to be fair. After I chewed out David so publicly and then marched him to HR to get fired, I think that everyone's a bit skittish and seriously considering the ramifications of office gossip, so people are a bit quiet.

Men no longer come up to bother Rose at her desk, which is a good thing. I see a few of the women tentatively coming up to chat with her, inviting her to join them at lunch, which I didn't see before. I think maybe between Rose's no-nonsense nature and the rumors the men were spreading, the women were annoyed and didn't want to associate with her. Now, luckily, that's changing.

I try to keep a lower profile and focus on work. I actually act like I'm dedicated to this job no matter how much I resent it. I shouldn't force Rose to always be the guard at the gate; and I want to remind my employees I'm someone who cares, not just the cranky asshole who will yell at them in front of their entire department. We have to be extra careful. I try not to talk to Rose in person, just emailing her what I need to, and keep the office door open—but handle things myself when I can. I wasn't thinking when I went to yell at David. I was just furious about how Rose was being treated, and I became protective.

Someone could do something with that. Someone might read into that. Especially if anyone noticed that I drove her home. N and I are close, of course, hell we still text all the time while I check up on her, but I haven't known Rose for nearly as long. People could realize that there's something more here if I'm not careful; and so for the next couple of weeks, I'm extra cautious.

It's fucking miserable, but it's how it has to be.

I keep thinking about how she climbed into my lap after I drove her home. I could feel myself getting hard, my cock hot and desperate pressing up against the fabric of my pants, my hands greedy on her body. I wanted her so fucking badly.

There's that voice in my head that keeps whispering, *you could just keep it out of the office.* As long as we only do it at home...

That's not going to work. I know it's not going to work. It'll bleed over no matter how hard we try to keep it compartmentalized. But fuck if it isn't a daily temptation. She's right there, she's *next door to me*, I could walk right over.

Fuck, if only.

The somber, tense mood only gets worse as the day approaches. It's always "the day" in my head. I don't know what else to call it. It's like even after all this time my mind still doesn't want to face it head-on and address it properly. Maybe because every day, I'm reminded about it. I can't move on when it's surrounding me; when it's the reason that I'm here in this office.

My phone buzzes at my desk and I answer it. "Hello?"

"Your mother's here," Rose says.

I look up and set aside the papers I'm reading. "Send her in. I'm going out to lunch so hold any calls for an hour."

"Of course, Mr. Chaucer." Rose's voice is quiet and she hangs up, making me wince. Rose isn't the quiet type. It doesn't suit her.

I put the phone down and my mother walks in. She's dressed in black. The rest of the year she wears whatever, but she always wears black on this day, like she's back at the funeral. "Simon, dear. You didn't tell me you had a new assistant."

"Yeah, Nadia's on maternity leave. She has to be on bed rest. That's Rose."

"She seems very sweet."

I almost snort with laughter but manage to turn it into a cough just in time. "Glad to hear it. She's been doing good work. Nadia trained her well."

"Pity she's your assistant," Mom remarks.

I just about choke on my own spit. "Excuse me?"

"Well, you could use a sweet, efficient woman like her. I did sometimes wonder about you and Nadia..."

"Nadia and I are just friends, Mom; we always have been." It was never that way between N and me, from the moment we met she was always more like a sister to me.

Mom hums. "Of course. I just wonder when you're going to stop sleeping around and get married, find something serious."

I sigh and grab my jacket. "Can we just go to lunch? I don't want to talk about this."

"Well, of course, it's just hard not to think about it on a

day like today." Mom smiles sadly. "Your father was always so excited for the day he'd have grandchildren."

I sigh. "I know." I gesture towards the door. "Shall we?"

"Of course. It's just I'm not getting any younger either… and neither are you, you know, Simon…"

"Mom, I'm not even forty. Frankly, I've spent enough time in my life doing what Dad would want." The words slip out of me, exhausted and angry, before I can stop them.

Mom turns around in the doorway of my office and stares at me. "What exactly does that mean?"

Ah, great. I square my shoulders. "It means I'm not going to have kids just because you and Dad wanted me to. I'm already taking over this company, aren't I?"

"This company is your birthright. Your father loved it, he worked so hard to make it what it is…"

"Yeah. He loved it. I don't. I'm doing this for *him,* do you really not understand that? Or are you that delusional? I know you're living your life stuck on Dad, but I'm not. I don't think I should. I'm sure as hell not going to raise a kid just so they can take over this company the way you and Dad did with me."

Mom's mouth drops open. "You don't mean that."

"Of course I mean it. I did what was expected of me. I took over the company. It's not my fault that Dad died younger than we thought, but I'm not going to rush into having a kid just because *you* want the family legacy continued, and *you* want to be a grandmother. In fact, I'm thinking I might not even have a kid at all."

"Simon!"

"I've done everything I was told to do! You're wearing black, Mom, like it's still his funeral."

"It's the anniversary."

"Exactly. I'm tired, okay? I'm tired. Every day for me is

the anniversary because every day I'm *here*. Doing *this*. My whole life has been doing what you and Dad wanted for me. I'm not going to bring a kid into the world just because it's what you want. I'm sick of doing what you and Dad want. He has more control over me now that he's dead than he ever did while he was alive and I'd laugh at the fucking irony of that if I wasn't so busy being *angry*."

Mom's cheeks are red and her eyes are wet, and I immediately feel like an asshole, but damn it I'm also angry. I don't want to take back what I said.

Mom doesn't even say anything. She just turns on her heel and walks away, clearly dismissing me.

Fuck.

I sit down on my desk and scrub at my face. I really didn't mean to make her so upset. It's not even that I don't want kids. My relationship with my father was a good one, and I'd love to be a father myself someday, I just don't want to have a kid *just* because that's what my parents would want.

I'm sick of doing things just because my father wanted it for me. Footsteps sound on the floor and I look up. Rose stands in the doorway. I open my mouth, then close it. I don't know what to say. Clearly, she heard everything. She steps in and closes the office door. Then walks over and wraps her arms around me.

I sink into her and hold her back, and let myself be comforted.

Chapter 17

Rose

It's honestly impossible not to overhear the argument between Simon and his mother.

It's clear from Simon's voice that he's in a lot of pain. I've argued a lot with Simon ever since I met him, and I could tell that he hates his job. But it also means I know what he's usually like when he's arguing with people, whether that's me, the board of directors, an employee, or someone else. He doesn't usually sound like this.

Simon is confident. He's always so certain that he's right. He's determined, and it can drive me crazy, but he's not someone who doubts himself. He argues because he believes that he's in the right. But not now, arguing with his mother, he doesn't sound like he knows he's right or seem confident in his opinion. He sounds hurt. He sounds tired. He sounds like he's lashing out.

I watch his mother leave. She doesn't even glance at me, but it's not like I blame her for it. She looks like she's trying not to cry. I get up and head into Simon's office, closing the door. It's probably a bad idea but hey, I'd want to give him privacy after that no matter what our relationship was. It's just that I'd close the office and stay on the outside. Now, I close it and stay on the inside.

Simon looks up. He looks so worn down, and oddly so *young*, so lost. I didn't think Simon was capable of being lost. I walk over and hug him, because I don't know what the hell to say. That seems to be the right thing to do, because Simon slumps into me, hugging me tightly.

I have to admit that it hurts to hear Simon say that he doesn't plan to have kids. I want kids, although I want to wait until my business is up and moving and sustainable. I don't know how Simon and I can have a serious relationship if that's something we differ on so greatly. But that's not a conversation for right now. Right now, the conversation is about Simon and his mother, and the hurt I can feel coming off him in waves.

"Let me get you some tissues," I murmur. I pull away and pull them out of his drawer.

There's something nice about this—me getting to comfort him after he comforted me. Even though I'm not happy that he's feeling hurt.

"Thanks." Simon sighs and sags back a little on his desk. "I'm sorry you had to hear all that."

"It's fine. I'm sorry that I overheard all that personal stuff. And I'm sorry about your dad."

"It was a sudden heart attack. We had no idea. He seemed to be in good health. One minute he was here, and the next..." Simon shrugs. "I had to take over everything."

"I know you hate it."

"Most people don't."

"Most people are stupid."

Simon barks out a laugh. "You would say that. I love it."

Butterflies flutter in my stomach. I ignore them. This isn't the time. "You're a good boss, though. I mean, you went up to bat for me, your assistant." I hold up a hand as Simon tries to protest. "I know, I know, you were also going a bit caveman on my behalf." I smile. "But if I was anyone else, would you have still gone to HR?"

"Oh, immediately. I would've fired David and had a talk with everyone in the company about the situation. It was unacceptable."

"See? You care. You gave Nadia paid maternity leave for the rest of her pregnancy while she's on bedrest and for the first year of the baby's life. That's above and beyond what most companies do. When Nadia was training me she kept warning me you were stubborn and cranky, but she also pointed out how much you care about making sure everyone here is treated well. She said you expect your employees to leave at five, and you don't want them to take work home. You're generous with vacation time and benefits."

I take Simon's face in my hands. "You're a good boss, Simon. I know you hate working here, but I don't want you to think that it affects your ability to run the company well. You care about your workers, and that's a lot more than most business owners can say."

Simon nods, still avoiding looking at me by staring down at the floor. "I appreciate it."

"You were there for me. I want to be there for you. Besides. Everything I said was true."

Simon pulls back in and wraps his arms around me, holding me tightly. I hold him back. He clearly needs it right now, and I want to do that for him. I want to be there for him.

My fingers card through his hair, and Simon softly kisses my neck. I don't want it to go any further and I don't think he does either. Not because we can't, but because that's not what this is about right now. I don't want to just have sex with him, I want to be there for him when he's having a bad day like this one.

"Just because you're good at this doesn't mean you should do it," I say, carefully. "I think you should also think about what makes you happy. You took care of your father's company and you're keeping it successful, but you shouldn't have to dedicate your entire life to someone else's dream. Just... something to think about."

I want him to be happy. I care, deeply, about making him happy.

"My mother would be hurt. This company is all she has left of my father."

"I don't think that's true. She has memories, things at her house—that's her problem and not yours. I know your father wanted you to take this company over but I think he'd also want you to be happy. I hope—if he was alive to see this —he'd realize... I don't know, I think we want something for our kids, and then when we see them do what we want and we see them miserable, we don't want that for them. I think he'd listen to you, if he were alive and you could talk to him about it. Nobody can say that you didn't try your best, that you didn't step up."

Simon's silent for a moment. "I'll think about it."

That's all I can ask of him.

"But thank you." Simon pulls back a little so he can look up at me. He smiles up at me. God, he's handsome. "I, uh, I had no idea how much I needed that."

I'll always be there, if you need it again. The words are on the tip of my tongue, but I swallow them down.

"It's been a while since I—well, N has always done what she could, but I haven't really let myself—let anyone be there for me. So thank you."

"What can I say?... I'm stubborn."

"And I appreciate it," Simon says, entirely seriously.

He's the first person who's appreciated that about me. He's the first person who's appreciated everything about me.

"I knew you wouldn't survive without me," I tease him.

Simon shrugs, still serious. "Maybe I wouldn't."

My heart speeds up a little in my chest and I hope that Simon can't hear it. This isn't just wanting someone sexually. This isn't just wanting to explore our relationship and see where it goes. We already have a relationship, and I'm invested in it.

"Maybe you should apologize to your mom, though," I add. "I... I get it. You have every right to be upset. But I think she was hurt. And on the anniversary... I don't know. I just know my parents and I have had a lot of fights, and you know how snappy I can get. You say things in the moment that you might not actually want to say. Words you can't take back... but you can make it better for having said them."

Simon nods. "I think it would be easier if I had someone to rely on. Someone I could kind of... talk to about all of this. It feels like everyone doesn't understand, or makes it worse. But you're right, I should say something." He smirks. "I'm a bit of an asshole."

"Hey, you've met me. Takes one to know one."

I could be that person for you, I want to say. I swallow it down. I want to be there for him when he has moments like this. I want him to be happy, and to help him get there. I want to be the person who sees Simon like this, me and no one else. I stare at Simon, my heart still pounding, and I realize that I want to be there for him always. This is so much more than I thought it would be. This is so much more serious than I thought it would be.

I'm falling in love with him, but I can't have him.

Chapter 18

Simon

I don't want to send Rose away, but she can't hold me forever; people are going to wonder what's going on. She goes to take her lunch. I order something delivered and stay in my office with the door closed. I'm not quite ready to see anyone else right now. I do feel better after my talk with her. Knowing that I am doing as much as I can and that my employees appreciate me helps.

I hope I wasn't too serious during our conversation. I didn't realize how much I wanted her, how much I *needed* her until Rose was holding me, and I was wrapping my arms around her and holding her back just as tightly.

Mother is there for me, I know that. But in this... she can't be. She doesn't understand. I have no one to go to. My friends are all rich kids who enjoy being rich and enjoy being powerful business owners. Nadia understood but it wasn't really something I felt comfortable getting vulnerable about with her. But Rose is there, and I can just collapse for a minute, and rely on someone else to hold me, for the first time since my father died.

I forgot how much I needed that.

It's hilarious, how Rose, the person I started out arguing with, is now the person that I trust and lean on—the person I'm vulnerable with. I guess it's our adversarial start that's led to this. I can be open with her about whatever I'm feeling because she started off seeing me at my worst.

I wish that I could do as she says. I know she's not giving me this advice lightly. Rose broke off from her family and is forging her own path, going after her dream, even though they don't support it. That has to be hard. She's not giving me some Disney-esque nonsense without understanding the consequences. I don't know if it'll really be worth it. Dropping everything to pursue my dream of owning a restaurant and working as a chef... what would happen to the company? Could my mother ever really forgive me?

Mom. I grimace. I do feel like shit for what I said. I shouldn't have done it, even if I do wish she'd understand the pressure she puts on me, the pressure I constantly feel from Dad even though he's dead and gone. I shouldn't have said shit that isn't really true just to hurt her.

I pull out my cell and give her a call, wincing. This probably won't be an easy conversation. Mom likes to dig her heels in. So did Dad. We're all stubborn assholes.

"Simon?" she sounds surprised, and I can't blame her.

"Hey. I... I wanted to call and apologize. I shouldn't have said those things."

There's a pause on the other end of the line.

It goes on long enough that I clear my throat. "Mom? You there?"

"I'm here, sorry." She gives a watery laugh. "I'm just surprised that you apologized so quickly."

Yeah, that's fair. I snort. "It's not really my thing, is it?"

"Well, darling, it's not really my thing either," Mom admits. "You get a lot of your stubbornness from me. I know your father loved the company, and he put everything into it. I would never diminish his accomplishments. But I flatter myself to think I had a hand in it too, encouraging him to go for it, supporting him through the bad early days. I wouldn't let him ever give up."

"And I'm glad you didn't." I mean it when I tell her that.

"But..." Mom prompts. "I know there's something else there, Simon."

Maybe it's time that I told her the truth. "You probably won't be surprised, given how things just went. But I do feel trapped here. I never wanted this life. I never wanted to take over the company. This was never my thing. I shouldn't have gotten angry the way that I did. I don't want to hurt you. I love you and I value our relationship. It's just..."

I can hear Mom sigh. "I know. I know and you took over everything from your father anyway. It was his dying wish and you've fulfilled it beautifully."

I want to ask her how much longer I have to fulfill it; if this is truly going to be my life forever; and if I'm never going to be able to be my own person. But I don't want to start another argument.

"I have to ask," Mom continues, "what made you apologize so quickly? I can't remember the last time you ever wanted to even admit you might be wrong about something."

Her tone is teasing, but curious, and I have to admit that she's right. I don't tend to apologize, just ask Rose. But that's kind of the whole point. Rose doesn't exactly apologize, either, and it's a clash of titans between us.

"I... I had a conversation with someone. And she pointed out that I might want to apologize to you."

"Oh? What kind of someone?"

"A woman," I admit. But I'm not telling her that it's my

111

assistant. "She's my next-door neighbor. I met her recently and we, uh. We had a rocky start but..." I chuckle fondly, unable to help myself. "I think you'd like her. She's a real firecracker. She's got no problem telling me when she thinks I've messed up."

"I'm glad to hear it." Mom pauses, then laughs. "I'm sorry, that makes it sound like I think you need to be told you messed up, and that's not what I mean."

"No, I do need that. And this person... she does that for me. She's as stubborn as I am."

"Good. And you—it sounds like you really like her?"

Mom's voice is so hopeful at the end of it. I can't dash her hopes just yet by telling her I can't be with Rose right now. Not after I just apologized and tried to make things right for my outburst.

"Yeah. I do. I'm kinda shocked by how much."

"I knew the right person would come along eventually."

Yeah, if only that person wasn't my literal assistant.

"You need someone who can change your mind and go toe to toe with you," Mom continues. "Your father and I were that for each other. We could both be so stubborn, but we respected each other and we tried to listen. As long as you do that, you'll be fine."

"Thanks, Mom, but it's early days yet."

"Can I meet her?"

"Not yet. I'd like to take a little more time, first." And not have my mom realize that I'm Rose's boss. "I don't want to put any pressure on her by going too fast."

"Of course, darling, I understand. But I hope you know that I'm happy for you. All that I want is for you to be happy."

Then let me give the company to someone else. Let someone else who wants it take over.

112

I swallow the words, as always. Mom wants me to be happy, but she loves my father and his legacy more. I've always known that.

"I want you to have what your father and I did." Mom's getting a bit choked up again. "That's all. I hope that you've found it with this girl."

"We'll see how it goes. But can I take you to dinner tomorrow to make up for today?" I can come up with some more information about Rose that Mom can hear, but that won't spell out that she's my assistant. And maybe by then, I'll even have something to say about the company.

Even as I think that, I know it won't happen. I haven't said anything to my mom about giving up the company so far, and I don't think I ever will. I don't know how I can permanently break her heart like that, my outbursts aside.

"That would be wonderful, Simon. Thank you. I love you."

"Love you too."

I hang up the phone and stare down at it.

Mom's happy for me, but only because she doesn't know the full story. It would be a very different tune she'd sing if she knew the situation Rose and I are in. I just wish that what I told my mother was real, and I could have Rose instead of just gripping my way white-knuckled through the days until I can be with her properly.

This can't go on. I have to do something. Rose needs this job so that she can get her company off the ground? Then fine. I'll make sure her company gets off the ground. I'm not going to stand around and wait for the universe to just be on our side any longer. I'm taking the reins into my own hands. I want Rose, and I'm going to have her.

Chapter 19

Rose

It's a Saturday, so I don't have work. Usually, this might mean I can relax, except that now it means doing work on my fashion business. Sewing clothes and modeling them, making sure the pictures are professional, posting them on apps, and trying to get a wide audience... it's another job.

I can't complain, though. It's what I want to do with my life, and besides, it keeps me distracted from the knowledge that I could just go next door to see Simon any time I wanted. It's hard to resist him, especially now that I've seen a more vulnerable side to him. I want to keep that soft side, safe.

He doesn't show that part of himself to just anyone, that's clear.

I want to be the person that he goes to when he's feeling that way. The fact that he listened to me when I told him he needed to apologize... it means a lot to me. I don't think he would listen to just anyone. I've seen how damn stubborn he can get, including with me.

It's so much harder now that I like him as a person, now that I know how much I'm drawn to who he is and not just how well he fucks me. I wish it was just sex. Just sex I could walk away from so much more easily. But it's not. It's spending eight hours a day with him in the office watching him be secretly unhappy and do a good job as a CEO anyway because it's what his mother wants and his employees need.

It's him protecting me and standing up for me and making it clear that no woman at his company is going to go through harassment. It's him wanting to impress me, encouraging my dreams, and liking that I'm sassy and sharp.

Better to focus on my fashion company and work my ass off on that, than give into temptation and show up at Simon's front door. I don't know that I'd be able to stay away from him if I didn't have something else to occupy me.

There's the sound of a car in the driveway and I frown, looking up. Could that be Simon?

My heart races faster. The thing is, if he shows up at my doorstep, I don't know that I can turn him away. I don't think I'm capable of that. But then I hear the click of heels on the front steps, and the jingle of keys in the front door.

I get up from the living room where I have all of my material spread out, and head for the foyer. "Hello?"

The front door opens and Chloe all but collapses inside, groaning with relief. "Oh, it's so *good* to be home!"

I can feel my brows shooting up and my mouth turning down into a frown. "What are you doing here?"

That sounds rude. This is her home, after all. It's just that I didn't expect her for a few more weeks and I currently have fabric and clothes all over her living room.

"Good to see you too," Chloe groans.

"No, I just—where's your boyfriend? What are you doing? Are you okay?"

"I'm fine, I'm fine, we just—ugh. He was *so* annoying." Chloe drags her suitcases inside and closes the door. "We went to the Coliseum and he was like, is this all we're going to do today? Like, dude, it's the Coliseum! Hello?"

She rolls her eyes and waves her hand in the air as if brushing off a gnat. "Anyway, I love partying as much as the next girl—ooh, and I got so many cute things shopping I can't wait to show you. I need a guy with some class, y'know? I'm thinking of joining one of those like, match-making sites, actually, the men are all older, but it means they're *mature*, y'know?"

I keep my eye roll to myself as I help her get her luggage upstairs to her massive walk-in closet. I'm not saying her boyfriend wasn't a dud. I can't even remember the guy's name. I just don't think that the guy's age was the problem. Or that Chloe's relationship problems will be solved by dating someone older. Then again, I probably shouldn't judge, given the situation I'm currently in.

"So, did you have fun while I was gone?" Chloe asks, tossing clothes out of her suitcases and throwing them haphazardly around.

"Uh. Been busy working. Got a job."

"That's good!" Chloe pulls out some other stuff and begins sorting her clothes. "I'm so glad. You know you can keep staying here if you need to. I hear minimum wage is like this whole thing now."

I blink. "Do you think I'm working somewhere and I make minimum wage? Where do you think I work, McDonald's?"

Chloe shrugs, hanging her new clothes on hangers.

"I work for the CEO of a pretty big company, actually."

"Oh, that's great! Y'know, there was this CEO we met up with in Paris…" And she's off, telling me all about her latest escapades.

I want to put my head through a wall, but I listen to her babble. It's harmless stuff; it's not like Chloe's going to be deterred. I'll just let her tell me all about her adventures.

"But anyway," Chloe wraps up, "Tell me about this job."

"It's really not that exciting. I'm just an executive assistant for a guy who owns a travel company. So they own resorts and things like that."

"Ooh, is he handsome?" Chloe heads downstairs and I follow.

"Why does it matter? He's my boss."

"Yeah, but he's not my boss. He's gotta be older to be a CEO, right?"

"He's actually not that much older than we are, he inherited it young when his father died unexpectedly."

Chloe frowns, seeing the living room. "What's all this?"

"Oh!" I grin. "Okay, so, this is the company I told you about. The fashion line? I got some advice to start on social media selling the clothes directly, in small batches, and work up my brand. Once I do that I can show investors that I'm a sure bet. I can get the money to open up an actual boutique as well as the online sales…"

Chloe nods, skimming over the living room with her gaze and then turning away. "Sounds fun."

I frown. "I mean, it's fun because it's doing what I love, but it's a lot of work."

"No, I'm sure it is." She heads for the kitchen. "Are you sure it's work you can do, though? Like, no offense but I know what my limits are y'know?"

I bristle. "Are you saying you think I can't run a company?"

Chloe shrugs. "It's just really hard. I've seen a lot of influencers crash and burn. People think that being an influencer is living this great life, but I've seen the other side. They go somewhere like to Europe, the way I did, but they spend their entire time finding these perfect spots to take photos, and they don't even enjoy where they are. It's honestly kinda sad."

I admit, that's a level of depth that I didn't expect from my cousin, but I'm a bit confused. "Are... are you saying that you think I won't succeed?"

Chloe gives me an odd look. "I just want you to understand how hard it is to get your business off the ground, even through social media. I think that you need to be realistic about what it takes."

"So you think I don't have what it takes."

"Well..." Chloe adopts a sympathetic look. "Honey, it's not like you've managed it so far, y'know? Don't you think that maybe you need to consider other options?"

Rage boils up in me. "Maybe I haven't succeeded so far because I haven't had any damn *support*," I point out.

Chloe looks surprised. "What do you mean?"

I lean heavily over the kitchen island. The same kitchen island where Simon brought me delicious cookies and told me that he loved my idea and believed in me and my business. I have to remember that. Simon didn't build the business he now runs, but he still had to keep his company afloat after the death of its original CEO and that's always difficult. People wonder how the ship will keep sailing when the original captain, the guy who built the boat, is no longer there. He originally planned to eventually open his own restaurant. Talk about a difficult business to start.

He believes in me. Simon knows what he's talking about. I can trust him, and that means I can trust myself.

"I mean, that you and the rest of the family don't believe in me. You've never thought that I could succeed. How am I supposed to get anywhere if I don't have any family to back me up? Maybe I'd actually get somewhere if you all weren't so convinced that I have bad luck, I'm not committed, and I'm on a fool's journey. If you guys actually helped me and supported me, I might get somewhere."

Chloe's mouth is open a little, like she's not sure what to say or what she's even heard. "I... well... we're just trying to... manage your expectations."

"Sure. That's fine. I can manage my expectations. But you guys just keep telling me I'll fail. That's not managing my expectations, that's *telling me you think I'm not good enough.*"

Chloe leans back a little against the counter, frowning—not like she's angry, more like she's thoughtful. "I suppose I didn't think about it that way."

"I know that you guys love me in your own way and want what's best for me, but you gotta stop telling me what to do. Let me do what I want to do! Okay? I'm not going to give up or change my mind. Wouldn't you rather I quit knowing that you helped me and were there for me; that I truly was able to give it the best shot I could? Instead of me wondering, 'Hey, maybe I could've made it, if I'd just had a little help?'"

I gesture around us at the massive house we're standing in. "You're my cousin and I'm never going to just ask you for a handout. But you have plenty of money to spare. You couldn't have ever, at any point, thought to give me a loan or become an investor in the company, so I had some financial cushion? Some way to help me get started? Everyone knows that the big problem with starting a business is getting the finances to pull everything together. You need seed money; you spend money when you're not making any at the beginning. You couldn't just... help a girl out?"

Chloe looks, to my surprise, genuinely upset. Shit, did I go too far? Have I hurt her feelings or made her feel like just a wallet? But then she walks over to me and pulls me into a hug.

I go stiff in shock, but then... I hug her back.

"I'm sorry," she whispers. "You're right. I wasn't thinking about it. I should've supported you."

"Look, I don't always approve of your boyfriends," I admit, pulling back a bit so that she can see my face. "But I'm not going to tell you to just give up on finding the right guy. I'm always going to tell you if I think the guy's a real scumbag; but otherwise, I'm going to say give it a try, right? You never know."

Chloe nods. She steps back and wipes at her eyes. "I'm sorry. I just had no idea how you felt. How we made you feel."

"I should've said something. You guys aren't mind readers."

"I just know that your parents worry, y'know? They worry about you and I get it. You have a whole family and support system back home and out here in LA you just have me. And I'm not. Y'know. Great." She gestures playfully at herself. "I'm glad you said something."

"Honestly, I might never have."

"What made you change your mind?"

I can't give away too many details. "I, uh, I met someone. He encouraged me to go for it; he told me that he believed in me and what I could do with my vision. It made me realize that all I needed was for people to support me.

He made me realize how unfair it was that you guys weren't doing that."

"Well, you don't have to feel that way anymore." Chloe takes me by the shoulders."I'll invest in your company, babe. I'll be your investor and you can get this shit *done*."

I laugh, giddy with surprise and relief. I really didn't expect her to actually invest, I just wanted her to know how much I could feel the lack of support. "Thank you, Chloe. You really are great, I hope you know that. Thank you for letting me live here and get my life back on track."

"Of course." She hugs me again. "I should've done more."

Then she pulls back again and heads for the fridge, grinning. "Soooooo... you met someone?"

I roll my eyes. "I don't want to talk about it."

"But you're gonna!" She grins and pulls some food out of the fridge to warm it up for dinner. "I want to hear all about him!"

"There's not much to tell." I have to be careful about what details I share. "We got off to a bad start since he's annoying as all hell, and he just does *not* like someone disagreeing with him. I don't think the guy's ever had someone stand up to him in years, but you bet I did, and instead of it annoying him—I mean it did annoy him but— he also liked it. He found it hot.

"He likes it when I tell people off for being assholes or being annoying. And he's protective of me. Some guy was bothering me, and he really ripped the guy. He believes in me, and I can't remember the last time someone did that. It's like we argue, but it's *fun* when we argue. He understands me." That's it. "He understands me, and I feel like he's the first person... who..." I stop. "What?"

Chloe's got this big, ridiculous, gooey smile on her face. "I don't think I've ever seen you like this."

"Like what?"

"Your face. It's like..." Chloe's smile grows wider. "Like you're in love."

I *am* in love. I'm in love with Simon.

Oh shit.

Chapter 20

Simon

When I open the door the next morning, confused, my arms are full of a happy Rose. "Good morning to you too, sunshine."

Rose hugs me tightly and then pulls back, smiling. "My cousin is going to invest in my company!"

"What!?" I wrap my arms around her waist. "Rose, that's fantastic."

I would've loved to invest in it myself, if that wouldn't possibly come back to bite us in the ass. I'm her boss, currently, and I'd like to be her boyfriend. It wouldn't look well for me to also be investing in her company. People could start a lot of malicious gossip over that.

"She came back early from her Europe trip, I guess the whole relationship didn't work out. Nothing new there. But she was saying... the usual things my family says about my idea, dismissing it; I don't know where it came from, but I told her off. I told her she needed to support me."

Rose takes my face in her hands and kisses me, like she just can't help herself. "It's because of you; I know it's because of you. You gave me that confidence. She actually listened to me and apologized, saying she'd invest in the company!"

"Rose, seriously, that's amazing." I spin her around, overjoyed on her behalf. "You deserve it. I'm so proud of you for standing up for yourself."

I force myself to let go of her and step away. We're at my house, not at the office, but I don't want to encourage too much.

Then I realize—what am I doing?

Rose has an investor now. She has someone to financially back her, and she can get her company off the ground. If she's doing that, then she doesn't need to work for me anymore. She can put in her two weeks and we can find someone else to replace her.

"I told my mother about you," I admit.

Rose's eyebrows fly up, and her mouth drops open. "You —you did?"

I nod. "I called her and apologized. She was, uh, kinda shocked I did it so quickly. I had to explain that you'd put my head back on straight."

Rose blushes and rubs at the back of her neck. "Well. I just don't want your stubbornness to get ahead of your good heart."

"Did you just say I have a good heart? Stop the presses! Call the newscasters!"

Rose rolls her eyes, but she's laughing. "You think you're hilarious."

"You have to admit, at one point, you never would've admitted that I was anything other than an emotionless, heartless asshole."

"No, I wouldn't have said that." She pauses. "I would've called you a stuck-up bastard who cared more about being right than being kind."

"There you go." I grin at her, and Rose grins back helplessly.

"You really do have a good heart, though. I know you care. If you didn't, you wouldn't be killing yourself at the company. You wouldn't be making sure that we don't over-work ourselves. You would have sold the company over to someone else as soon as you could. You would've gotten as much money as you could out of it, and you wouldn't have cared if the new owner drove the company into the ground."

I stare at her. In all of my time, I've worked hard to use my prickly nature to make sure nobody knew how much I hated my job. But it also meant that people didn't know I actually cared about my workers. Only Nadia's ever gotten close to me, and she's my friend. I care about her, of course I do, but it's different. Rose sees me in a whole different way. And when she talks to me like that, I can't help it. I want her so fucking badly, and I'm sick of not having her.

"Well, I told her about your heart. About how you take me to task when I need it and you don't let me get away with being too stubborn. I told her about how I hadn't felt this way about someone before."

"Your mom mentioned that you... that you have a habit of sleeping around."

"I did. Not so much the last few months. I've been busy with..." I gesture around us.

Rose grins. "Tearing your house to pieces with your own two hands instead of hiring professionals?"

I smirk. "You're never going to let it go, are you?"

"You can afford the best contractors and workmen, people who are *trained* in this stuff..."

"I just wanted to do something with my hands, let me live."

"No, I think killing you is a lot more fun."

"Then you should do it over dinner with me."

Rose's face drops into shock. "Simon..."

"No, I mean it." I take her by the hips and pull her into me. "Listen. You have an investor now. That means you can get your company started properly, right?"

Rose nods. "I don't want to take too much advantage of Chloe's hospitality, but she said I can still stay with her, and she's going to foot the bill on my business expenses. I would still like to chip in how I can; help buy groceries and stuff, but..."

"But you can find a less demanding job for that, one that might pay less."

She nods.

"So that means you can put in your two weeks. You won't be my employee, and we can go out." I squeeze her hips lightly. "I really, really want to take you out. I want to actually give this a try."

"You sure that you won't..." Rose clears her throat. "You won't get bored? Once you can actually have me..."

I shake my head. "If I was going to get bored with you, then that would've happened the first time we had sex. I was a one-and-done kind of guy; once I had someone and it was fun, I moved on. I didn't have time to get attached. But I just want more of you. Every time we spend the day together... I love it. But I hate that it's while we're at work and pretending we're nothing to each other. I can't touch you how I want. I can't be open with you the way I want to."

I grin at her. "Don't you think if I was going to get sick of you I would've done it by being stuck in the office with you day in and day out for weeks?"

Rose snorts with laughter but puts her hands over mine and gently pushes my hands away. "But what if, once you have me, it changes? What if it's just that I'm the forbidden fruit?"

"You weren't the forbidden fruit when I first asked you out," I point out. "And how will we know until we try? Let me take you out. Let me show you a good time on that date I promised you all those weeks ago."

Rose takes a deep breath. "If you're sure..."

"I'm sure. Rose, I'm so damn sure. Let me take you out and spoil you. You deserve to be spoiled. You've been working your ass off for me and building your own damn company. You've put up with harassment and gossip. I think you deserve a damn break. Let me be the one to give it to you."

Rose's whole face lights up. She really is gorgeous, I've thought that ever since she stormed up to my gate and started bothering me, but now, with her looking so damn happy... she's even more beautiful than before. I want to make her look that happy all the time.

"Okay," Rose tells me breathlessly. "Okay."

Finally, *finally*, I pull her in and kiss her. "You're the one thing that makes me happy at that damn place," I admit. "The rest of my life is just... doing what I'm supposed to do and taking care of the company, upholding my father's legacy. I started working on this damn house because I was trying to give myself something meaningful outside of work to accomplish. Something that wasn't being a playboy."

Rose's hands slide up my chest and wrap around my neck, her eyes warm with understanding.

"But you make me happy. You actually make me *happy*. I can't remember when I felt that way before my father died. So I want to keep you, if you'll let me."

"If I'll let you." Rose laughs. "All right, big boy. Spoil me and take me out to dinner."

Then she sobers up and kisses me softly. "You're the thing that makes me happy, too. I'm going to miss working with you, only because I'm going to miss seeing you that much every day."

"Hey, I'll be happier outside of the office, though."

"That is true."

I want to kiss her and pull her against me. I want to pick her up and carry her to my bedroom and fuck her the way I've been dreaming about for weeks... but I hold back. I promised her a proper date and so far we've only been able to have sex. I don't want to trip at the finish line and make her think that I'm not serious about this relationship.

Instead, I gently push her back. "I'll see you later. When I pick you up for our date."

Rose smiles and lets me push her, steps back even, giving us more space. "I look forward to it. Mr. Chaucer." She winks at me because she can't resist being a cheeky little minx, and it's part of why I'm falling for her. Then she turns on her heel and hurries out the door, and I'm left standing there with a dopey grin on my face, one I didn't think I could even have.

Things are finally looking up.

Chapter 21

Rose

I feel like I'm floating.

I've never felt this way before. I've dated briefly; my last one was while I was still in school, but it was never as serious as I'd hoped it would be. I would keep waiting for that big emotion that everyone talked about, that giddiness, that bone-deep conviction, and happiness.

When it never came, and the relationship fizzled out, I just... moved on. I never had too much investment in the first place, so it didn't break my heart when it ended. I just felt disappointed, every time, that I didn't care more. I had started to think that spark that everyone talked about, that giddy floating feeling, didn't really exist.

I told myself it was fine. I had a company to focus on. I could worry about dating and finding someone to marry, I could worry about my other dreams, after this first dream was completed. But now, I know how it feels. I know it's real. I understand that feeling of 'cloud nine' for the first time.

Chloe is going to invest in the company. I'm going to actually be able to get my dream off the ground. And that means I can be with Simon—Simon who's taking me out on a proper date.

I know this is a risk. I'm still technically working for him as his assistant. I haven't quit yet, but I think it'll be okay; honestly, I just can't wait anymore. We've been so good this whole time, resisting temptation, and it's been driving me crazy. Even more so now that I've seen so much more of who Simon is.

It's worth it. It's worth him.

Simon's date is a Tuesday. I'm not sure why he picked that day, he just said it would be easier. I do think that it's a good idea we don't go out on a Friday or the weekend, that's more of a typical "night out", just in case someone Simon knows sees us. Simon doesn't tell me anything about what we're doing or where we're going. My blood thrums with anticipation as I leave the office for the day.

"See you tomorrow, Mr. Chaucer," I say, gathering my things.

"Of course, enjoy your evening," Simon calls from his office, apparently still lost in paperwork.

I struggle to keep the grin off my face as I head to my car. Simon's tone was so calm and dismissive, I don't think anyone could have any idea how he really feels about me. In fact, I might have doubted myself, if I couldn't remember the way he let me hold him, the way he clung to me, and how eager he was to take me out on this date.

Simon's good at hiding his feelings from the world. It makes me feel special that he shares the truth only with me. I drive back to Chloe's place. She's out, which isn't surprising. She's been doing retail therapy to get over her relationship and, as promised, she's signed up for all those matchmaking sites, so she's got several dates lined up, too. All the men on these sites are rich, apparently, and it makes me laugh inside to think that maybe Simon might be the kind of person people would hope to meet with these services.

Too late, I can't help but think. *He's mine.*

It thrills me. I've never been somebody's or had somebody be mine before, never thought of it like that, but the idea that I see a part of Simon nobody else does.... he sees a part of me... it has my stomach filling with butterflies. I'm a cliché, and I don't care.

Simon hasn't told me anything about what we're doing, but I feel like he'd warn me if we were going to do something that would require a specific outfit, like hiking boots. I pick some flat shoes anyway, just in case, and a dress I've made myself that I wouldn't mind walking around or doing some light activity in. I hope I look cute. I hope I look like I'm worth it.

Cold fear stirs in my gut. I'm not rich. I don't come from the same world as Simon. What if, once he actually has me —once I'm not shiny and new or someone who just gets his blood pumping from the argument—he finds that I'm not all that he wants? I don't know his world, I'm not sophisticated enough...

There's a knock at the door and I jolt, trying to control my breathing. Simon doesn't care about my economic status. He's encouraged me in my business, and he's protected me when others have tried to tear me down. I have to believe in that. I can't let myself get cold feet now when I'm so close to having what and who I want.

I head downstairs. "Coming!"

I open the door and let out a shuddering breath. Simon's standing there in a dark red button-up shirt with the sleeves pushed up and the top few buttons undone; a pair of black jeans hug his legs and remind me just how thick he is every-where —how strong and broad he is.

His gaze drops down and then slowly scans up my body and I feel myself flushing. "You look beautiful," he murmurs.

I tuck a strand of hair behind my ear. "You don't look too bad yourself."

He also doesn't look too fancy, either, so I know I made the right choice in my outfit.

Simon holds out his hand and I slip my hand into his, letting him lead me out of the house. "Where are we going?"

He grins at me as I lock the door and then follow him, my hand still caught up in his, to his car that he's parked in the driveway. "You'll see. I wanted to give you the date I originally promised you."

I can vaguely recall him saying something about thinking I came from a rich family and so wanting to do something different, wanting to impress me with something I hadn't experienced before. But he knows now that I'm not used to fancy, expensive places. Maybe he's changed his plans, then, I don't know.

"You're lucky I trust you," I point out.

Simon chuckles as we get into the car. "You trust me, huh? We've come a long way. Pretty sure you wouldn't trust me to even die properly in the beginning."

"I wouldn't have trusted you with construction, that's for sure."

Simon grins and pulls us out onto the street. "You can always come over and help, you know."

"Absolutely not. Sewing is where my work with my hands begins and ends, thank you very much."

"You should give it a try. You never know, you might get into it."

"Or, consider, I could just get myself a nice tall glass of lemonade and watch you do all the work."

"Oh, I see how it is. You want to just ogle me. You want me for my body."

"Oh, no, you found me out." I grin at him as we pull onto the Pacific Coast Highway. "I got the job as your assistant just because I wanted to give you blue balls every day, didn't you know?"

"Hey, I wouldn't put it past you after that first day."

"I would've considered it, but that would've been torturing myself, too."

Simon nods sagely. "Yes, being unable to have sex with me must've been torture for you."

"I was referring more to being stuck with your personality for eight hours a day, five days a week."

Simon laughs, big and full, and the sound slides through my body, making my chest feel light. I have that floating feeling coming back. It's not arousal. It's something so much more dangerous.

It's love.

"You know, we're going to confuse the hell out of people, going on like this." He's watching the road so he can drive, but he keeps glancing over at me, like he can't help himself; like he wishes he could just stare at me forever. "The two of us arguing as if we hate each other."

"Hey, people will pretend to be strangers in bars and role-play for their anniversaries. I'd say that this isn't the strangest thing anyone's ever done."

"Touché."

He pulls us into a parking lot off the highway, and I

realize we're going into the fancy stone-paved driveway of a restaurant.

A valet opens the doors for us and we get out. "You must be Mr. Chaucer," the man says.

"Yes." Simon hands the keys over. "Thank you so much for doing this."

The valet grins and shrugs. "Well, you picked a good day, we're not super busy on weekdays at this time of year."

My brow furrows. "What is he talking about?"

Simon takes my hand again and walks us over to the entrance, where I can see a beautiful courtyard for the restaurant, ringed in by a low wall that keeps people from falling off but doesn't do anything to block the magnificent view of the ocean.

I gasp a little, the view is truly amazing. Simon smiles softly at me, like that was exactly the reaction he was hoping for from me.

There's a young woman at the host stand, dressed in a black blazer and smiling at us. "Chaucer, party of two?"

"That's us." Simon's still looking at me.

"Well, normally this is the part where I'd consult our floor plan and tell you to follow me right this way..." The host grabs two menus. "But clearly, that won't be necessary this time. Why don't you pick whatever table you'd like?"

A suspicion forms in my mind as Simon leads me through the restaurant and sweeps his arm out. "Go on, pick whatever table you want."

"Did you buy out this whole place?" I hiss at him.

Simon grins. "Just pick a table."

I pick a small two-top table that's right at the back edge of the restaurant. It has a truly amazing view—the blue of the ocean is entrancing—it'll give us the perfect setting for sunset.

"And yes, I did," Simon answers me, pulling my chair out for me. "I told them I'd cover the tips and pay of whoever was scheduled to work tonight, and pay the owner as much money as he expected to make this evening. I didn't want them to lose any money by hosting us. I figured on a weekday there would be fewer reservations to cancel."

"You just... bought out a restaurant."

"Yup." Simon sits down and the hostess hands us our menus.

"Your server will be out momentarily to talk to you about the wine selection," she says, and then she gives us a wink and leaves us to it.

"She's probably going to play games on her phone the whole time while we're up here," I whisper.

Simon grins. "I'd hope so. It's not like she has anything else really to do."

I can't quite believe that he did this, just for me. Just to impress me. "You know you didn't... have to do this, for me."

"I know that. But I wanted to do something special for you and I feel like we've had enough time interacting around other people and holding ourselves back, don't you?"

Simon reaches across the table and gently takes my hand. "You're worth doing special things for. You're worth that extra effort. I didn't want to take you to a place that everyone knows and half the reason you're there is clout. I didn't want to take you somewhere that felt like I was just showing off my wealth. I wanted to give you something beautiful and private. That's why I bought this place out. Now we can enjoy this lovely meal just the two of us."

My heart melts and I'm pretty sure my face is on fire. I squeeze his hand. "Who knew there was a massive romantic lurking under all that bluster and crankiness?"

"I think I was just waiting for you to bring it out in me."

"Careful, keep saying things like that and a girl's going to get a swelled head."

"Good. You could do with some self-confidence."

"Is that so?"

Simon sits back as our wine menu is brought and we chat with our waiter. I look at the menu and we order, and then we're left alone again.

Simon looks at me intently. "You have no problem arguing with people when you know they're wrong, and you're great at standing up for yourself. But you shouldn't have to do it all alone. I know that you can take care of yourself, but I'm saying that you don't have to. You deserve support—from your family, from your friends and coworkers, and from whoever you're dating. And I'd like to support you, however I can.

"I can't throw money at you. I'm still your boss and then I'll be your boyfriend if you'll have me. I wouldn't ever want to endanger your professional integrity. But I want to make you feel special. You deserve that."

My sight gets blurry and I look away, out over the ocean, so I can take a moment to compose myself.

"Nobody's ever talked about me like that before," I admit after a moment.

I dare to look back at Simon, who looks about as vulnerable as I feel. It hits me that as open and raw as I feel about this, someone doing all of this for me and supporting me and saying this to me... he's putting himself out there, too. He bought out a restaurant for me. If that's not commitment then I don't know what is.

I can't leave him hanging.

"Well, that's their loss," Simon replies.

"Your loss that people don't see this side of you, either," I point out.

Simon pulls back as the food arrives. "It's easier when— thank you—when I just cover everything up."

"Being in the office?"

Simon gives a wry smile. "Would you believe me if I said my classmates in culinary school used to love my sense of humor?"

"I can believe that, actually."

"I'm not saying I was a completely different person, but I was happy there. I was happy as a chef, and I don't want my employees at the company to deal with a miserable boss. It's none of their business and it's not their problem."

"But don't they deserve to see what I see? The caring part of you?"

Simon's silent for a moment. "Maybe."

I take his hand again and squeeze it. "You feel that you owe your parents. I understand that. And maybe I'm the wrong person to talk to about this because I left my family to pursue my own dream. I didn't feel bad about it, it was never something that I questioned as... something that I owed them. But my relationship with my family is rough and it sounds like you were really close with your father."

"We were. I always knew he wanted me to take over and I never wanted to; I just thought I'd have more time. I thought he was so healthy. I figured I'd have time to get my own career going and have a few years of owning a restaurant under my belt before Dad started to think about retiring. By then I figured I could... talk about it with him and convince him to let me stay away from it and he could find someone else to take over."

"But then..." I trail off.

Simon nods.

137

"I just think, if your father loved you the way it seems he did, he would want you to be happy, more than anything else."

Simon smiles, a bit sadly. "I would hope so. But I never got the chance to talk with him."

"I hope you'll think about it."

"I will." Simon clears his throat and gestures at his food. "Now, I've got to get you to try the paella..."

It really is nice to have the whole place to ourselves, joking and laughing without worrying about being over-heard—or having to raise our voices to hear each other over the conversations of others. The view is amazing, and we get to watch the sunset without interruption.

Afterward, I think maybe we'll go back to Simon's place or he'll drop me off at Chloe's, but instead, he drives us past that, into Beverly Hills.

"Where are we going?"

Simon grins. "Questions, questions, questions."

We park and get out, and he pulls something out of his wallet while he leads me into the Rodeo Drive shopping area. It's a black credit card.

Simon holds the card out. "Go ahead." He nods at the various shops. "Go nuts."

"What do you mean?"

"You're a woman who appreciates fashion, but you probably can't afford the kind of things you usually want to buy, and I want to change that. Go shopping, and buy what-ever you want."

I stare at him in shock for a moment, my jaw dropped open. He can't possibly be serious, telling me to go wild on Rodeo Drive of all places. Just purchasing one item here will be hundreds of dollars.

But Simon just keeps smirking at me, no guile or teasing

in his gaze. Just pleasure, like he's excited and happy for me to do this.

"Your funeral," I warn him.

"I think I'll be able to take it," he quips.

At first, I feel like I'm in a dream. I can't really actually be able to afford this stuff, right? All these lovely clothes and accessories that I've idly looked at in magazines and in runway videos, but knew I couldn't ever afford… and now I actually can.

I try not to spoil myself too much. I don't want to take advantage of Simon's generosity. I just get some things that I think will be helpful for me to have when I'm meeting with potential other investors and fashion professionals so that I look like I'm successful and on their level.

Still, it's so fun to walk into these fancy stores and know that I *can* buy anything I want. I'm not coming in here "just to browse" and feeling like I'm a bad person who's going to get caught out for it. Like I'll be thrown out because I'm not spending money, and the salespeople are glaring at me the entire time.

Instead, if I don't buy anything, it's because I truly am choosing not to. Simon encourages me to take a good look at things, to try clothes on if I want to, and just the very sight of him has salespeople gaping in awe and envy. I don't know that they know exactly who he is, but Simon just looks like someone who's important. And they can clearly tell that he's the one who's got the money. I'm the person choosing what to buy, but he's got the purse strings.

I don't mind that people know. It's not like they're going to see me around here again unless Simon brings me, and it's not as if I'm some young twenty-something with a much older man calling him 'Daddy', clearly only with him for his money.

Simon's eyes light up when I try on clothes. I keep trying to tell him that he doesn't have to watch me try things on, but he shakes his head and insists that he likes seeing me happy like this.

"You can't tell me you're this interested in fashion," I point out, holding two different purses up to see which one I like better.

"I'm not. But I'm interested in seeing you happy. I'm interested in what you're interested in. You care about this, that means I care about it."

"And yet you didn't care that you were waking me up at an ungodly hour of the morning."

Simon laughs loud enough to startle a few other people in the store. "You're never going to let that go."

"You don't want me to let it go."

"That's fair. I don't." He eyes the purses. "The green one, by the way."

"Oh? Really?" I hold up that purse.

"It compliments your eyes better."

That has me blushing, but I get the green purse. When we finish, and get back into the car with our purchases in the trunk, I fully expect Simon to take me home and turn us north up to Sunset Blvd. Instead, he takes Wilshire and heads east.

"Where are we going?" It's already eight in the evening and dark out, where else could we go?

"You'll see."

He drives us into downtown. We park and get out, and he leads me directly into an area that I know well: the Fabric District.

I can feel a grin stretching across my face before I can stop myself. "Oh my God."

The Fabric District is a place in the LA Fashion District

140

where people are open at different times. Some are open early and you want to get there to get the good fabrics, but others are open late.

Simon shrugs. "I figured you could use some more supplies for your company. I can't back you as an investor, but I can help you purchase more fabrics."

I grin and get to work, Simon dutifully holding whatever fabrics I hand him as I haggle with the various older women, many of them with English as a second language, who run the shops.

The dinner at the fancy restaurant and shopping on Rodeo Drive were nice and they made me happy. But I have to admit that shopping in the Fabric District, explaining to Simon as we go along what I'm looking for and what clothes I'll turn the fabric into—as he listens with a small, fond smile on his face— makes me the happiest.

If he's not careful, I'm going to get used to him looking at me like that, and then I'll really be sunk. By the time I finish getting everything I want, it's late, and we're hungry again, so we put everything in the car and then stop by a taco truck, eating delicious, messy tacos in a parking lot while leaning against the side of the car.

"Did you like today?" Simon asks, his voice soft.

"I did." I lean against his side. "Are you enjoying the tacos?"

"Oh God, you bet." Simon grins. "You know, Los Angeles isn't exactly a slump when it comes to the restaurant scene but I think that the best food, the real Los Angeles food, is in taco trucks and stands like these. You gotta find the hole-in-the-wall places to really get the best food in the city."

"I'll be honest, I wouldn't have expected it of you."

"I know, classically trained chef, I get it. But these

people know what they're doing. They've been raised in this kind of thing, and you don't have to go and get a degree in cooking to be good at it. The fact is most people don't. They just start working at a restaurant and work their way up." Simon's the most relaxed I think I've ever seen him, leaning against the back of the car, his shirt rumpled, a smile teasing at the corners of his mouth. "Did you ever know about Jonathan Gold?"

"No."

"He was a food reviewer for the Los Angeles Times. He talked once about the Michelin guide coming out for Los Angeles and how it was made by cowards too afraid to venture more than a few minutes from their Beverly Hills hotel."

Simon's clearly quoting from memory. It's adorable.

"That's not how real Angelenos eat, he said, and he was right. He said the guide should be ignored unless you were a French businessman visiting the city and terrified of the 'teeming masses'." Simon snorts with amusement. "He understood where the real good food in a city is."

"Would you want to open your own taco truck?"

Simon chuckles. "No, not really my personal style. But I'd want something approachable, something low-key. None of these insanely fancy-tasting, menu-type places. Maybe something like a gastropub."

"Sounds fun."

"I haven't thought about it in ages."

"Why not?"

"I didn't see the point if I wasn't going to ever get to do it."

I lean against him, resting my head on his shoulder. "You know that you didn't need to take me out to Rodeo Drive or buy out a restaurant to impress me, right? I loved it, don't get me wrong, but my favorite part was doing this with you. And it seems like this is what you really enjoy doing."

I reach down to take his hand and squeeze it. "I don't need you to impress me, Simon. I don't care about your wealth or your prestige. I just like spending time with you." I pause. "And arguing with you."

I can't see his face with my head resting here like this but I can still tell that he's smiling down at me. Silence reigns for a moment as we watch other people getting in line to order from the taco truck. It's an eclectic mix of construction workers who want something on their way to an early start to work, and women in tight short club dresses who want something to eat after a night of partying, and a few tired businessmen who stayed too late at the office.

"That's what I love," Simon says quietly. "Dad loved giving people vacations. He loved being able to create this... paradise for them, this place away from their normal world and they could just let everything go."

He jerks his chin towards the taco truck. "What I love is bringing people together with food. All these people are from different walks of life and normally won't interact, but here? Here they're all the same and enjoying the same food. It unites people like nothing else. When I cook for people, I feel like I'm showing them love."

It's the kind of sentimental, earnest, sweet thing I never would've expected from Simon when I first met him. It makes my heart ache, makes me want to take his own bruised, hidden heart and hold it in my hands, cradle it, and keep it safe. Simon puts his arm around my shoulders, and I feel safe, in turn. I feel like I could tell him anything.

It's funny how we started out yelling at each other, but now, just standing here in silence... it's not awkward to just exist with him. To breathe in the night air and observe the city.

"I like that about you," I murmur. "I like all of you, Simon, the real you. I don't like your money or who you have to pretend to be. I like who you are. Even the parts that might not seem pretty."

Simon turns to look at me for a long moment, something in his eyes that I can't name. Then he says the three words that I've been feeling in my heart, but never would've expected—

"I love you."

Chapter 22

Simon

I have the time of my life spoiling Rose. I know I didn't have to go all above and beyond with her, yeah, but I don't care. I wanted to give her the best time. I didn't want to deal with the usual rich people bullshit. I wanted to give us privacy, and a beautiful early dinner. I wanted to give her all the things she wants but can't afford.

I want to make her happy. But when Rose tells me she likes the second part of our evening in downtown better than the first, I can't help it. I have to tell her how I feel.

This is the part of me that I know the other people in my social sphere would roll their eyes about if they knew. There are people who know I was in culinary school before I came and took over my father's company. I'm sure a lot of them think it was a... youthful whim, so to speak—the kind of thing that young people, freshly adult, do because they want to forge their own path and feel independent from their parents.

Others, I think, understand I was serious about it, but picture me being in some fancy place, becoming a well-known chef like Wolfgang Puck, the kind of person who owns restaurants that people spend months waiting to snag a reservation. That's not me, though. I was excited about my work at a Michelin-starred restaurant in New York City before I had to come back and take over the company. It was going to be an amazing learning experience. But I want something that's more casual for my own restaurant. I want people to feel like anyone could get a reservation, and anyone can come on in and be family. I want to have a place that feels like a second home, no matter who you are.

I want the food to be damn good, and who gives a damn where the chefs got their experience? I don't care if they went to France or have some kind of degree. I care that they understand the food, that they're steeped in it. Nobody that I have to rub elbows with on a daily basis will understand. They care about the name on the door; they care about everyone knowing exactly where they ate; and they care about the zip code of the restaurant's location. They don't actually care about the food, and they prove it every time a new fad enters the picture and they swarm over to that and abandon whatever it was they swore was so amazing before.

Even before she says anything, though, I notice that Rose seems so much happier in the Fabric District than on Rodeo Drive; as much as I can tell, she had fun there. She picked out some careful statement pieces in Beverly Hills, a purse, a dress, and a couple of blazers—things that I noticed will help her look sophisticated and are the kinds of things you wear to an upscale business meeting or luncheon.

In the Fabric District, though, I loved watching her as she ran around haggling with the various shop owners; as she ran her hands over fabrics; and as she grinned with delight taking photos and writing notes on her phone.

I don't know the first damn thing about fashion, but I sure do know what it looks like when someone's happy and in their element. I just like watching Rose be happy. I like watching her do what she's good at and I like listening to her explaining things to me. Honestly, I feel like I could watch her work all day and not get bored.

When Rose tells me that she prefers me like this, prefers this side of me, I can't help myself. The words well up in me before I can stop them and I blurt out, "I love you."

Rose stares at me, her eyes wide with shock.

I grimace. "That's. Not how I planned on saying it. In the parking lot by a taco truck."

"So you planned on saying it?" she asks, her voice breathy.

"I did. I wanted to wait, I didn't... this is our first official date. I didn't want it to be too soon, I didn't want to make you uncomfortable."

Rose is blushing, her face lit up from the neon signs of the taco truck and the streetlights that dot the area around us. She looks almost starstruck. "Well. This might be our first official date but it's not like we didn't know each other at all before this. We've spent a lot of time together."

"Forty hours a week, in fact."

She laughs. "Yes."

"You don't have to say it back, by the way. You don't have to do anything. I just wanted to tell you." I clear my throat. "You see me, and I don't remember the last time someone really did that. To be fair I... I don't know the last time I even *let* someone do that, not even N and she's my best friend, in a way. But you see me. And I can't stop feeling this way."

"You support me like nobody else has, Simon. You see me, too." Rose wraps her arms around my neck. "How am I supposed to not fall in love with you?"

Ava Nichols

A shadow passes over her face before I can kiss her, and I wrap an arm around her waist. "What?"

"I just didn't think you'd feel the same way, that's all." Rose winces and I can see her face get pinker as she blushes harder. "I didn't want to... I didn't want to hope or assume... I mean, with everything..."

"You should. You should assume."

She smiles up at me. "Then don't worry. I'm falling in love with you and it's actually kind of scary."

"You're kind of scary yourself."

"You bet I am."

I pull her in and kiss her. "I'm taking you back to my place," I murmur against her mouth.

The drive back to my place feels like torture as the anticipation builds. Rose puts her hand on my knee, and it slowly moves up as we get closer and closer to the Bel Air neighborhood. At least at this time of night, there's not a ton of traffic so it doesn't take us long.

I'm tempted to pull over and have her in the car, but I don't want to risk us getting caught for public indecency. Besides, I want to finally have her in a real bed, instead of on the floor or outside or against a desk. I want to do this right. This is the woman I'm in love with. She deserves no less.

We get to my house and pull into the drive, and I'm out like a shot. Rose stares up at me, her eyes wide and lips parted. As I open her door for her and pull her out of the car, I can't help myself, kissing her again, pressing her up against the side of the car. She looks so cute, in a pretty dress, her hair loose around her shoulders. My hands slide up her legs to her thighs, and she hops up a little with a gasp, her legs wrapping around me.

"Loved you in this outfit," I murmur.

"I made it myself."

"Damn right, you did." I kiss down her neck. "You're going to be a success, Rose, I just fuckin' know it."

"Oh, yeah, talk dirty to me," she teases, but I feel her arch up against me. Yeah, she can pretend all she wants, but she likes the praise.

My cock aches in my pants, and the temptation to fuck her right here, right now, is so fucking strong, I feel like I can taste it in the back of my teeth. But I pull back, even though it feels like dragging myself through molasses, and I force myself to take Rose by the hand and guide her to the house instead.

Luckily, I haven't touched my bedroom in the renovations yet, focusing on the downstairs and the opposite side of the house. I get Rose inside and flick on the light so that we don't trip over anything, and then our mouths are colliding again. She's so fucking soft and warm against me, and my hands roam greedily over her curves. I'm always greedy for her, but this time, there's no need to rush. There's no sudden, overpowering shift from anger to lust. It's been building all evening and I can take my time.

Rose gasps as I kiss down her body, pulling down the straps of her dress and falling to my knees at the same time so that I can bring the dress down with me. The fabric falls away and the sweet expanse of her skin is revealed for my hungry mouth.

I kiss down her body, and Rose falls back against the bed as I get between her legs, licking at her through the fabric of her lace panties. "You dressed up for me."

"M-maybe," she admits with a gasp.

God, I could spend hours on her body. I keep biting and licking at her, exploring the curves and angles of her body, until I can hike her thigh over my head and toy with her through her lace.

Rose's hands fly to my hair and she whimpers. "Simon, please..."

"Please what?" I pull back enough so that I can pull her panties off.

Rose stares at me for a moment like she's forgotten what she was going to say. I see her swallow hard. "I want you naked, too. I want to see you."

How can I deny her when she asks me in that sweet tone of voice?

I stand up and quickly get undressed, then dive back into her. I kiss her hard, my body rolling against hers. Fuck, it feels so fucking good to have our bodies together like this, no clothes in between for the first time. We get lost in it, Rose wrapping her legs around me, the two of us rolling our hips lazily as we kiss and kiss and kiss.

I can't remember the last time that I was slow with sex like this. When I was sleeping around, then it was all about the rush. I was in and I was out, it was the rush of conquest, and it was fun but it wasn't something I lingered over. Now, I want to linger. I want to take my time. I'm not trying to hurry to the finish line. This feels like a marathon, not a sprint.

I have no idea how long we kiss for. Our bodies intertwine like twisting snakes, but eventually, my hard cock drags against her folds, and I can feel how hot and wet she is.

Fuck, she feels so fucking good.

Rose whimpers into my mouth and I drag my cock against her again, deliberately, almost but not quite sliding inside her. "You want this?" I murmur. "You want me to slide inside you?"

"Yes, yes, *please,*" she whispers. Her arm wraps around my shoulders, her nails digging in. Her legs spread, her knee pushing up, inviting my cock to slide right inside her tight, wet heat.

I move my fingers down to dip inside her. I don't want to hurt her. I don't want to be too rough by accident. Oh my God, she's so fucking wet. Holy shit. I groan. "You really want this, huh, sweetheart?"

Rose whimpers helplessly. I curl my fingers inside of her and she cries out, shuddering. "Y-yes, yes!"

"That's a good girl, tell me what you want." My voice is a rough purr. I scissor my fingers, making sure she's nice and open for me. Rose writhes on my fingers and grinds down onto them, like she's trying to get more of me inside of her.

I rub my thumb against her clit and she cries out, shaking. "Oh God, Simon, *please....*"

It's so tempting to get her off right now, just like this, but I decide to draw back. I want her to come on my cock tonight. I want to draw this out. Rose moans as I pull my fingers away and line up my cock inside. I'm not thinking, not at all, just about the fact that we're finally in my bed and I get to have her—and I slide inside.

Fuck. *Fuck.*

I take a moment to breathe, my mouth open, my head hanging down heavily between my shoulders. I look up, glad I can see Rose's face. I don't want to miss any expression as we do this. She stares up at me with slick, parted lips, her face flushed with desire. She's absolutely beautiful. I could stare at her for hours, if I wasn't throbbing with heat and need.

Rose forms the word *please* but no sound comes out, her voice stolen. I get it. My own damn voice feels pretty stolen too. I shudder and let my eyes fall closed, then brace myself and pull partly out, thrusting back into her.

Rose arches her back and my eyes fly open so that I can watch her react. I brace one knee and bring up her legs around me so that I can thrust into her deeper, and she claws at my arms, gasping and writhing on my cock.

She's perfect. Goddamn.

I have to stare at her as I fuck her, caught up in how beautiful she is, how hot she is, how fucking lucky I am. I've had a lot of sex in my life. It's not a brag; it's a fact. But I've never felt connected with someone during sex the way I feel with Rose.

I kiss her ferociously, my hand under her thigh to keep her leg up as I thrust wildly into her. I know when I get the angle just right because Rose cries out into my mouth and bites my lip. I growl and keep at that angle, fucking her hard and fast as her cries get increasingly desperate.

"You gonna come for me?" I growl, kissing all over her throat and neck, up her jaw, biting and tugging lightly on her ear. "You gonna come on my cock, sweetheart?"

"Yes, yes, yes," Rose chants, her nails digging into my skin. "Oh, fuck, *yes*..."

She clenches around me; I feel that heart-stopping rush as she comes, shuddering underneath me. I lose all control. I groan into her breasts, fucking her in short, sharp thrusts, like I'm trying to crawl inside her and never come out. In this moment, I wouldn't mind it. I wouldn't mind being completely intertwined with her always.

This is the woman who lets me be myself. We started out with her seeing possibly the ugliest part of me, my prickliness, my stubbornness, my refusal to back down. Now she knows the vulnerable parts of me, the parts I never show anyone else; and I know she'll keep them safe. I drive into her, again and again, the orgasm building from my toes and through my body until I spill over, gasping into her skin.

Rose moans as I come inside of her. I feel her fingers reach up to comb through my hair.

For a moment we lie together, getting our breaths back. Unlike every other time, there's no reason to pull away. We're not outside and we don't hate each other. We're not on the floor, or in my damn office where anyone might find us.

We're in my bed, safe in my home, and we have all night.

I push myself up a little to kiss her, stroking her sides as Rose's fingers continue to run through my hair. She looks sated and satisfied, and I feel so fucking content I almost don't know what to do with it. I've never felt anything like this before. I just know that I want to keep it.

"Stay the night?" I murmur.

I've never asked someone to do that before, but Rose is pulling it out of me. I meant it when I said I felt this way about her. I'm falling in love with her, and I can't seem to stop, and I don't want to. I want to hold onto this safe sensation, this soft joy.

Rose smiles at me and brushes our noses together. "Yes," she whispers.

I can't remember the last time I felt actually happy, and she's the one to thank.

Chapter 23

Rose

This sex isn't like the other times.

We take our time, kissing for ages before we actually get to the main event. Simon's hands on my body are possessive without being rough, exploring; it's almost like he's never had me before. It almost feels like the first time, like we've never done this before. It's all gentle and new. The way that Simon couldn't stop looking at me the entire time... the way he stared at me with this look of almost awe on his face...

It was what pushed me over the edge. I've never had anyone look at me like that. I didn't know it was even possible for someone to ever look at me like that. From the moment he looked at me and said I love you, it felt like something in my chest had cracked open. I feel vulnerable and exposed in a way I never have, but it's okay. It doesn't scare me because the way that Simon kisses me and holds me tells me he's feeling the same way.

We take our time, not having to rush, not caught up in a sudden flood of anger and lust. It all feels softer, but also sharper, everything in technicolor. I swear I can feel my orgasm building throughout my entire body, like I'm slowly stepping deeper and deeper into a lake and I want to drown.

Drowning in this is glorious.

Coming around Simon's cock feels so damn good, and then he comes inside of me and that feels almost better because I feel like we're connected in every way possible. I don't want to move afterward. I feel like I could fall asleep just like this, kissing him into gentle oblivion.

"Stay the night?" he asks, as if I want to do anything else; as if there's anywhere I'd rather be.

We kiss for a while longer, but eventually, we do have to pull apart before the mess becomes more than we can handle.

"Okay," I give in as Simon leads me into the bathroom, "if you chose the shower yourself then I'm impressed. You get one point."

"Just the one? After everything? You're a harsh judge."

I grin and slip past him to turn on the water. He has an amazing rain shower with glass walls and tile done up in shades of blue that make abstract shapes on the wall.

Simon presses a button on the wall, and the lighting goes from the brightness it held when we first walked in, to a muted yellow, as if lighting the room with candles.

"Romantic."

Simon shrugs. "What can I say? You bring it out in me."

The water's nice and hot so I step in and Simon follows me under the water. I'm immediately entranced by the way the spray from the shower hits his skin, and how it slides down his shoulders and chest. I reach for the soap so that I'm not just staring at him, and I hear the snick of a bottle cap being opened.

"Mind if I wash your hair?" Simon murmurs.

I tip my head back to let the water fully hit my hair and wet it all over. "Not at all."

A sigh escapes me as Simon's fingers slide into my hair and he massages my scalp. He's methodical and firm but gentle, and I find myself leaning back into him, trying not to go boneless. Simon hums, pleased, and continues to wash my hair until he rinses all the shampoo out from the strands. When he finishes he tips forward and kisses my temple, and another sigh slips out of me. He takes such good care of me, and he wants to take care of me. I don't know that anyone's ever wanted to do that in a way that didn't make me feel patronized.

"My turn," I murmur, pulling away and picking up the soap and washcloth.

I wash him all over, taking my time to enjoy every dip and curve in his muscular body.

He really is fucking gorgeous. I don't know how I got this lucky, but I do know I'm not letting him go. We dry off and climb into Simon's gigantic bed together. It's so soft and comfortable, and I can already feel my eyelids drooping. I smile into the pillow.

For the first time, since I left my parents' house to move out to Los Angeles and give this whole thing a shot, I feel like I'm home. Of course, there is the slight issue of this not being my home.

Chloe's a late sleeper, thank God, so when I wake up in Simon's arms in the morning, I don't feel like I have to immediately run out the door. It feels good to wake up with him, to feel held and warm, but I can't let myself linger too long. I have coffee, and he insists on making me breakfast. Of course, it's delicious because Simon's a damn good cook; and then I'm out the door and sneaking back to Chloe's.

I'm sure Chloe will still be asleep, but that doesn't mean I want to wake her, so I open the front door quietly and slide it closed very, very gently. I'm still in my dress from the night before but luckily she didn't see me go out in it. So, even if she's nursing a hangover in the kitchen, she won't know immediately I'm doing the walk of shame...

"Rose? Is that you?"

Shit. She sounds alert and awake. Way too alert. I set my purse down and walk into the kitchen, where Chloe is waiting with two mugs of coffee. Oh God, she's been waiting for me.

What the hell? "Hey, Chloe, what are you doing up so early?"

"It's not *that* early, aren't you usually off to work by now?"

Simon had sent a message to my work email telling me to come in by 10:00 am since he would be out of the office this morning, as a cover for why I'm heading in late, but Chloe doesn't know that. "Yeah, but you don't like to get up before noon."

"Fair enough." Chloe sips her coffee. "I just wanted to have a quick chat with you to see if you could clear something up for me."

"Okay." I sit down and sip the coffee. I already had a cup but hey, what's the harm in one more? I feel like I'm going to need it.

"So, I had a visitor yesterday. I was hoping to talk to you about it but you never came home."

"Oh?" I can feel my voice threatening to crack.

Chloe nods. "Yeah, very weird, it was this older woman. Mrs. Chaucer, she introduced herself. She was so happy to meet me, she just couldn't wait to get to know me so she had to come over and say hello. I thought it was like some weird new neighbor thing. But then she said that she had to meet the woman who was dating her son."

My jaw drops open. *Shit.*

Mrs. Chaucer. That's clearly Simon's mother. Simon mentioned he'd told his mother about me; he must've told her that I was his next-door neighbor. So his mom comes over and says hello to the person who lives here... which is Chloe, not me.

Oh my God.

"So, is there something you want to tell me?" Chloe asks. "Because last I checked I sure as hell am not dating my next-door neighbor. Isn't he the weirdo who's doing construction all the time on his house? The whole neighbor-hood's going batty over it, but apparently, he's terrifying so nobody says anything. I think he's lost his mind."

"Uh. I might have. Started something." I wince.

"What do you mean?"

"I mean that his damn construction woke me up, so I went over and gave him a talking-to, which he didn't appreciate, so we got into an argument... and one thing led to another."

Now Chloe's the one with wide eyes and a dropped jaw. "And you had sex!? And now you're dating!?"

I wince as her voice hits an octave only dogs are supposed to be able to hear. "Something like that."

My mind is racing even as I try to stay relatively nonchalant on the outside. I've talked to Chloe about my work. If she puts together that my boss is the next-door neighbor... especially now that she has the last name. It wouldn't take much for her to realize that "Chaucer" is also the last name of the CEO of the company where I work.

I can't let her find out I'm dating my boss. I don't think Chloe would report me to the company HR or anything, God no, but she's terrible at keeping secrets most of the time. She'd let it slip somehow and then I'll be up a creek without a paddle.

"And he told his mom about you?" Chloe recovers herself and whistles before sipping at her coffee. "Damn, it must be serious." She pauses. "Wait, is that why you didn't come home last night?"

Luck really is not on my side. Maybe my family has a point and I am unlucky after all. "I thought you wouldn't notice."

"My date was disappointing so I came home early. I was all set and excited to dish to you, and then... you weren't here and you didn't come home last night."

"You could've texted."

Chloe snorts. "Oh, please, I figured you could use the fun. If you were out somewhere I was sure it was fine; you're the responsible one out of the two of us. I was just glad you were having fun, wherever you were. But then this woman shows up acting like I'm her son's girlfriend, and I didn't know what to say or how to tell her she was mistaken. She was pretty damn sure that it was her son's next-door neighbor, and that's what I am, so..."

"I'm so sorry." I put my head in my hands. "I had no idea his mom would meddle like that. I know that she's a bit. Uh. She's opinionated. So's he. But I didn't think she'd come barging in like that."

"She seemed excited." Chloe shrugs. "Y'know, glad her son had finally found someone. I'm pretty sure I saw tears in her eyes at one point."

"Oh, *God*." I grab my phone to text Simon.

I have to warn him about what his mom is up to.

Because if she ever sees me at Chloe's and then remembers me from Simon's office... and *now* she thinks that *Chloe* is Simon's girlfriend...

We're so screwed. We need to figure this mess out. *Quickly.*

Chapter 24

Simon

I really didn't think about how good it would feel to wake up with Rose in my arms.

My house has felt pretty empty and cavernous lately, but I figured that was because I'm in the middle of renovating it. I don't have an exterior wall downstairs on the south side of the house, so of course it's going to feel cavernous and empty.

It's not until I have Rose sharing my bed that I realize it's not the construction that makes the house feel that way. It's my loneliness. With Rose here, the house finally feels cozy. No construction is required.

We have breakfast and I make her shakshuka. The noise she makes when she first takes a bite has me nearly bending her over the table again, but I catch myself in time. I don't want to let the food go cold because I couldn't control my cock for two minutes.

Rose notices, though, because she winks at me. I grab a coffee and my own plate and sit down with her. The breakfast is lighthearted and casual. If I had any lingering concerns about how we'd be together the morning after, in the cold light of day, this is chasing them all away.

She teases me about the ongoing construction work. "I have to say, I was surprised at how well I slept. Given that we're basically in a glorified barn."

"What would you like, then?" I shoot back. "If you were to live in a place and renovate it."

Rose thinks about that for a moment. "I do like the idea of something rustic. I think I'd want something a little more... nature-inspired in theme? Similar to Art Nouveau."

"Art Nouveau, huh?"

"Yeah, like John William Waterhouse."

I grin at her. I don't say it out loud, but I find myself thinking, *guess I gotta go look up Waterhouse, then.* Rose does have to go, though, before her cousin wakes up. She's not ready to tell her and I'm fine with that. Until Rose is no longer my assistant, we have to be extra careful. I don't think her cousin's going to rat us out but it's one of those things where the more people know, the more likely it is for that information to fall into the wrong hands.

I clean up breakfast and then throw the sheets from last night into the washing machine, and then I just pour another cup of coffee and sit down on my front porch. There's a stillness inside of me that I haven't felt in ages. The last time, in fact, was when I was in the kitchen at the restaurant where I'd gotten a job out of culinary school. It was a busy shift, but I hadn't been frazzled. Instead, I'd felt this sense of calm settle over me. I'd just smoothly flowed through everything that needed to be done for all the orders.

The head chef of the place had complimented me at the end of my shift and told me that having a good state of mind was what I needed to make it in the restaurant industry; and that a good chef wasn't the yelling stereotype. I tried to carry that leadership and that sense of calm into my work at my father's company, but I couldn't ever find it for myself. I've been running around, taking on projects like redoing my damn house, chasing that sense of stillness until I forgot it was even what I was chasing in the first place... it was that far gone from me.

Now it's back, and I know it's because of Rose. Thanks to her, I'm feeling content. No need for distractions. I can just relax and exist.

Then my phone buzzes. I pick it up. It's a text from Rose. That's odd. I don't think she forgot anything here at my place but if she did, wouldn't she just come back over to get it? I open up the text.

Your mom came over to see Chloe yesterday. Apparently, she thinks Chloe is your new girlfriend.

I nearly drop the phone. What the fuck!?

I'm so sorry, I text Rose back. *I have no idea why she did that. She likes to meddle with everything. As you noticed at the office. I'll talk to her and I'll get back to you.*

Jeez... I call my mom.

"Simon! Darling, I was just about to call you. Well, in a short bit. I wouldn't want to bother you at the office."

"Of course not." She bothers me at the office all the time, but... "Mom, I wanted to talk to you about something."

"Actually, dear, I wanted to talk to you about something, too. I just met your next-door neighbor."

"Oh, good, because that's—"

"She's all wrong for you, I was shocked that she was the woman you'd mentioned to me."

Oh boy. "Mom..."

"No, no, I know that you'll protest but I just want to get my two cents in briefly, let me say what I want to say and then you can say what you want to say, all right?"

"All right." This will be interesting.

"I'm not saying that she's not a lovely person. She was very kind to me and had me in. She got me some coffee and we chatted. It's just that she's far too shallow for you. I mean… there's nothing wrong with loving the high life. Goodness knows, I love it. And she seemed to have a keen interest in travel. She told me she'd just been to Europe recently. Your father and I loved to travel together."

"Uh-huh."

"But the way she talked about it… it didn't seem to be your style. She struck me as the kind of girl you'd have a one-night stand with, not the kind of girl who would actually be good for you in the long term."

"Mom…"

"I'm glad she was able to talk some sense into you the other day and that she stands up to you. You need a strong-willed woman like that, but I'll be honest: I didn't sense much of that from her when we spoke. She seemed very lost although I doubt she'd appreciate it if I told her that. You need someone who really knows who she is and what she wants out of life."

Mom's voice lowers to a conspiratorial tone. "And while she certainly has enough money of her own, I very much got the impression she's looking for a bit of a sugar daddy. Don't let her take advantage of you!"

I'm biting the inside of my cheek hard to keep from laughing. "Uh-huh."

"You're such a hard worker, you always have been, you need someone who has that drive. Remember how you were going to open your own restaurant? Someone like that."

"Yeah. Mom, I agree with you."

"Don't get stubborn with me—what?" Mom's passionate

defense is halted in its tracks as she realizes what I just said. "You—you agree with me?"

"Yup."

"But... you seemed so serious about her. Did she say something? Did she tell you I came over? Did you two have a fight?"

"No, Mom, I agree with you that the person you spoke to is the wrong woman for me because she's the wrong woman, period. That's not the woman I'm dating. You spoke to Chloe, right?"

"Yes."

"That's her cousin."

"But she said she lived there?"

"She does. Her cousin's been staying with her while she gets her company off the ground. Trust me, she's very driven and independent. She takes things seriously in life. I think you'll really like her."

I can feel the stress melting off Mom's shoulders. "Oh, I'm so glad to hear it. I didn't want to talk down about someone you cared about, and I was so excited you were looking into seriously dating finally... I hated to ruin it... but she really just didn't seem right for you."

"She's not." I grin. "I promise. But you have to promise me something in return."

"I'll be perfectly nice when I meet her."

"No, Mom, I want you to promise not to meddle. Okay? Do not try and meet this woman before I choose to introduce her to you. Do not ask me more questions about her. I want you to meet her. I really do."

I'm surprised to find that when I say that, I mean it. I actually do want her to meet Rose. I have no idea how it'll go. But I love my mom even with how she drives me crazy. I love Rose, and I want them to meet. I think Mom will like her, or at least appreciate Rose's drive.

"But I'm going to introduce you to her on my own terms, when we've had a little more time to be a couple. Okay?"

There's silence on the other end of the line, but it doesn't feel like an angry or hurt silence. "I understand. I might have been... a bit overzealous."

"Maybe just a little. But I promise that I'll introduce her to you. I think you'll like her."

"Good. And I promise I won't meddle any further."

Thank God. "Great. Thank you, Mom, I really appreciate it."

"Just don't let it take too long for that day to come, all right? I'm anxious to meet this girl who's done so much for you."

"I promise, Mom, I won't let it be too long."

Not when I'm feeling this strongly about Rose.

I want to be realistic. I never thought of myself as a romantic before, but I guess watching my parents while I was growing up, and seeing how much they loved each other, did something to me that I didn't even realize. I don't want to rush things with Rose and ruin our relationship as a result. But without even realizing it, I came to view this as something long-term. Something serious.

I just hope that she feels the same way. You can say you love someone, but that doesn't mean that you're ready to marry them, or that the reality of the relationship won't change something. I have to be careful.

"Good." I can hear the smile in Mom's voice. "I love you, sweetheart. I just want the best for you."

"I know. I love you too." The best for me would be to

leave the company, but that's not what we're talking about... and it's not going to go anywhere.

The moment I hang up, I hurry to get ready for work. Rose is probably already on her way there, so I don't want to call and distract her. I'll just deal with it when I get to the office.

Sure enough, when I arrive Rose is already at her desk, typing away and handling the various memos and calendar updates. "Rose, you got a minute?" I ask, heading into my office.

"Yeah, I need to show you the modified schedule for the week..." She picks up some papers and follows me into the office.

I leave the door open since I've made such a policy of it since Rose was hired; if I close it now that might seem suspicious, but I talk in a low voice as Rose puts the papers on my desk. "You need to put in your two weeks."

"Now?"

"My mom tried to meet you and ended up meeting your cousin."

Rose shudders. "I know. I was worried that she'd tell Chloe stuff that would make Chloe realize you're my boss. I've tried not to tell her much about you, as my boyfriend or my boss, but..."

"I understand." I sigh and rub my temples. "My mom was definitely grilling me earlier about your cousin. She was telling me to break up with her."

"I'm sure that was very hard for you to do," Rose says soothingly, a smirk lurking at the corners of her mouth. "But Chloe will get over it, don't worry."

I snort in amusement. "Oh, good. I'd hate to think I broke her heart."

Rose gives into the impulse and lets her smirk spread

across her mouth. "Would you like me to give you my two weeks now, boss?"

"Maybe not in this meeting since I called you in. How about you give it to me tomorrow? You'll probably need to talk to HR as well."

Rose nods. "I'll get on that. And I'll make it clear that it's nothing you or anyone here has done, this is a great place to work. I've just gotta quit for personal reasons."

"Very personal reasons."

She rolls her eyes, but she's smiling. "You're ridiculous. I can't believe I ever thought you were witty."

"Aren't you lucky my mouth's good for other things, then?"

"Oh, true, I guess I'll keep you around after all." Rose taps the papers she put on my desk. "Take a look at the new schedule. I'll talk to HR tomorrow morning."

Tomorrow morning then. Only two weeks that we'll have to wait, two weeks more of pretending like we're just boss and employee, practically strangers although friendly ones.

Two weeks, and then I can finally, finally have her.

Chapter 25

Rose

Two weeks really isn't that long, or so I tell myself, but it feels like an eternity. I'm sure that the whole situation with Simon's mother and Chloe has something to do with it. Simon's promised me that his mother isn't going to meddle any further, and she'll be patient about meeting this new mystery woman in his life; nonetheless, I worry. My parents sure never can resist the urge to give me their opinions and meddle in my life whenever they can. It's why I went all the way across the country to get away from them.

Chloe's not dumb enough, either, for this to slip past her for long. I just have to hope that she's so distracted by her own problems that she doesn't decide to turn to my life as a source of entertainment. Chloe's not a bad person; she just doesn't realize how often she views everything as just a fun round of gossip and drama. Maybe it is for her, with her money and social status insulating her from real consequences. But for me? This could be devastating.

I just try to keep my head down at work and carefully

avoid mentioning anything at home, other than the fact that I've put in my two weeks.

"Since you'll be my investor," I explain, "I can get a more part-time job that won't put so many demanding hours on me, so I can still help you with groceries and gas; then this business will be my full-time job."

Chloe's okay with that. I think she can see how much I don't want to take advantage of her and make sure I contribute to the household, so I'm not some kind of free-loader. Luckily, this means she has no reason to wonder about why I'm quitting. Nobody at work knows anything either other than I'm off to start my own business. I've kept to myself, anyway, especially after what happened with my male coworkers, so nobody has a hold on any real gossip.

I start interviewing replacements, first by calling up the women who were considered for the position along with me by Nadia. I'm sure most of them have found other jobs by now; but if any of them want to quit, or are available, they've already made it to the last round of elimination. I think I can trust Nadia's judgment on one of them being a good fit for Simon.

Even though I'm sure that everything's fine, and there's no need to worry, I still find myself feeling like I'm under a microscope. I know, intellectually, that nobody's checking up or wondering about me. And I know that nobody really cares all that much about why I'm quitting, but I still can't help feeling sick over it.

It's so bad that I don't want certain foods anymore that I usually like. I find myself craving junk food and ice cream late at night instead, like I'm on a post-breakup comfort food binge.

And when I'm not craving junk food, I'm feeling like I may need to throw up. There's just this sick knot in the pit of my stomach, like on that first day of the flu when you feel almost as though gravity doesn't quite work on your stomach anymore, and everything just feels *wrong*.

We're so close to the finish line. We just have to stick it out for two weeks. Fourteen days. But as those days tick on by, I feel worse and worse. Could it be that I only want Simon when he's forbidden fruit? I worried that was how he saw me all this time, but he's all in, or at least he's doing a good job of acting like it. I haven't felt any hesitation from him. He gave me an amazing day, a beautiful date, and he told me that he loved me. Am I the one who's actually got cold feet this whole time?

I think about getting to hold his hand and spend more time with him. I think about going out for more dates where he takes me to the kind of food places that only a true food lover would know, where we chase down food trucks and hole-in-the-wall restaurants. I want to eat with him on street corners and parking lots as we watch the city go by. I want him to show me all the places in Los Angeles I wouldn't even think to go, and I want to turn around and show him all the places he wouldn't think to go, either.

Hell, I want to go shopping with him and have him hold my bags; just having him there, even if he doesn't know nearly as much about fashion as I do, makes it all more fun. So... no, it's not that I'm getting cold feet. I want Simon. I want him badly.

Then why do I feel so sick?

It's not until I find myself nearly falling asleep at my desk, and then struggling to get up the next morning that I realize it might not be nerves. I might actually have the flu. I feel weirdly lethargic and emotional. I mix up something on the calendar, in a brain fog, and I nearly burst into tears at my desk. I have to go and cry in the bathroom about it.

I'm not the type to cry like that. I stare at myself in the mirror in the bathroom for a minute, carefully wiping up my face, so nobody can tell. I am utterly confused. Mistakes happen and I fixed it quickly, so what gives? It has to be the damn flu.

I feel terrible about calling out because I need to be at work, but I just can't find the energy and focus, and I don't want to pass the flu on to anyone else. Chloe makes me some classic Campbell's chicken noodle soup with crackers. It's basic, but I appreciate the gesture. It reminds me of when I had a cold as a kid and my mom would take care of me.

"How're you feeling?" she asks as she watches me eat.

"Fine, just nauseous and tired. You know how it is."

"Yeah, I get it. At least you don't seem to have a fever." Chloe's face changes to one of alarm.

"You okay?"

"Yeah, uh, be right back."

I eat quietly and respond to a few *hope you feel better soon* texts from my coworkers. When Chloe comes back, she's dressed for the day and grimacing. "Everything good?"

"Yeah, I, uh, just started my period."

"Oh *no*."

"Yeah, it's fine." Chloe laughs. "Amazing how it's something we get every month and yet it sneaks up on me constantly. You'd think I'd be on top of it by now."

I open my mouth to tell her that I'm lucky because mine's pretty regular—and that's when it hits me. My stomach churns, but not with nausea. It's genuine anxiety and fear this time.

My period hasn't arrived. I discreetly check my calendar on my phone. The last time I got my period was... shit, way too long ago. I definitely should've had it by now. I get it every five weeks like clockwork, and now I'm a few weeks late?

My mind races over the last couple of weeks as I recall the way I've been feeling. I thought it was the flu or something similar, but I don't have a fever, sore throat, or cough. My sinuses are fine. I feel like I'm *about* to get the flu, like those first couple of days, but the symptoms… the weird cravings, the nausea, the lethargy… those are all symptoms of morning sickness, too.

I struggle to keep my face neutral as I finish eating. "You know, I think it would be good if I went for a short walk. Get some fresh air."

It won't be a "short" walk to head to the nearest store that'll have pregnancy tests, but I can't ask to borrow the car or admit where I'm going, or Chloe will be suspicious. I don't want to tell her in case I'm wrong. I could be wrong. I really, really hope I'm wrong.

"Are you sure?" Chloe frowns. "If you're not feeling well…"

"No, I know, but I'm well enough for a little walk, and I haven't really been outside as much as I'd like to be, work and all. I'll walk and then take a nap and rest."

Chloe doesn't look totally convinced, but she shrugs. "All right. I'm going off to hang out with some girlfriends, you let me know if you need anything, okay?"

I smile at her. "I will, I promise. Thank you."

It might not be much from a lot of people, but Chloe going to make me some canned soup is a lot coming from her. Once Chloe's out of the house, I take a quick shower, get dressed, and head for the nearest drugstore.

The south of Bel Air bumps up against UCLA. There is a gas station I could walk to over to the west by the 405, but I worry that the guys there might recognize me since

I've stopped by there to get gas a few times in Chloe's car. Not that it's really anyone's business what I buy, but I'd rather not take the chance they say anything to Chloe.

UCLA it is. Nobody bats an eye as I walk through campus and stop by one of the on-campus drug stores that supplies various conveniences to students. I pick up a box of pregnancy tests and walk back to the house. By the time I get there, I'm exhausted, which is almost a good thing. It means I'm too tired to panic. I take the test and then hop in the shower to clean off the sweat, so I'm not just sitting there spiraling while I wait for the results to register.

I get out and stare down at the little stick resting on the sink counter. It's just a little device, and yet, it feels so menacing right now. I swallow hard and force myself to go over and pick it up. It's a big fat plus sign. A positive. I pull out another test and take that one, too, just in case. Just to be sure. I get dressed and come back to check it.

A plus sign there, too.

Fuck.

I sit down hard on the edge of the tub, my heart pounding in my chest. I should've been more careful. I should've been on birth control, or asked for a condom, or both. But all of our times having sex except for the last one were reckless moments of abandon, swept away by emotion. Besides, it's really too late for the whole... would've, could've, should've routine. What's done is done. We were reckless, and now here we are. Or rather, here I am.

What am I supposed to do now?

Chapter 26

Simon

I'm worried when Rose calls in sick. It's probably nothing, although I check and make sure nobody else at the office is feeling crappy. But it nags at the back of my mind all day, especially whenever I look out and see her desk empty. She's fine, of course she is. Not everyone is my dad. It's rare, even, for what happened to Dad; there one moment and gone the next. Rose is fine. There's no reason for me to freak out. I'm just protective of her.

When I finish up my work day and head home, I still haven't gotten a response from Rose on how she's doing. I'm sure it's nothing. She's probably sleeping and has her phone on 'do not disturb'. But...

I stop by the grocery store. I can cook up some food for her, something hearty and healing. A nice soup for example. From what Rose has told me about her cousin I'd be shocked if Chloe enjoys cooking or even really knows how, and Rose herself shouldn't be cooking when she's sick. I doubt she's got enough food really saved up ready to eat. Some home-cooked food will do her good. Help her feel better.

Normally, I'd worry that I was overstepping. I'd never do this for a random employee, not even if that employee was my assistant, or for a neighbor I didn't know well. But Rose and I are past that; we've been so damn careful, we need to keep being careful, but... it can't do harm just to show up as the next-door neighbor and give her something.

Nothing suspicious about it. People don't even know she lives with Chloe.

I load up my cart with groceries and head home, then get to work. I make a few different soups, nothing too creamy or thick since she'll need help clearing out her sinuses, and some heartier dishes for when she's feeling on the mend. Then I load it all up in containers and put it in a reusable grocery bag and walk over to Chloe's house.

Heading over to drop off some food, I text Rose so that she knows I'm coming.

I don't get a response. When I knock on the door and ring the doorbell, it takes a couple of minutes to get a response. It's Chloe who opens the door, and I'm not super surprised. I'm sure Rose is in bed. But that doesn't mean it's not disappointing.

Chloe frowns at me. "What is it?"

I hold up the bag. "I made some soup and food for Rose, to help her feel better."

Chloe's face does something strange, like she wants to soften but can't let herself. "You made this?"

I hand the food over and Chloe takes it, peering inside the bag. "Wow."

"I might have gone a little overboard."

Chloe narrows her eyes at me. "So you're the guy, huh?"

"Uh. Maybe?" Depends upon what Rose has said. "Can I see Rose? Just stop by and say hello?"

Chloe shakes her head. "No. Sorry. She's uh. She's contagious."

Something about her voice is odd, but I can't place it. I'm not sure what she means. But Chloe's a stranger, so it might not mean anything at all, and I'm just reading way too much into a simple situation.

"I understand. Just... make sure she gets the food, okay? And she's having electrolytes?"

Chloe smirks at me. "You're cute."

I bristle a little. She makes it sound like I'm the nerdy freshman offering to do the hot cheerleader's homework. "Just make sure she's okay."

Chloe rolls her eyes. "Yeah, trust me, she's gonna be fine. Not that it's any of your business."

Then she closes the door in my face. What the hell? No wonder Rose has such a rocky relationship with her family if this is how they behave. Chloe's a... well. She's a piece of work, that's for sure. If all of her family is like this then I'm not surprised that Rose has developed such a sassy, fighting instinct.

I head on back to my place and let things take their course. Rose is going to feel better on her own and while I want to pamper her, at the end of the day the real thing that helps healing from the flu or a cold is lots of rest and fluids. I got her the fluids, and she's got to just rest now.

Besides, she probably doesn't want Chloe to see us interact and realize just how close we are or that I'm her boss. We're so, so close to being free that it would be stupid to trip at the finish line now.

I try to focus on construction at the house and on work while I wait for Rose to feel better. She's out of the office for a whole week when I get the notice on my calendar—her two weeks is up.

She's free. She quit.

I focus on finding her replacement out of the finalists that Nadia considered hiring when she picked Rose. It's annoying as hell to find a replacement, but I do what I have to and select someone I think will do a good job at the task. If not, hey, I'll just find someone else.

Katya is polite, but not a pushover, she has lots of experience, she's efficient, and best of all I have zero attraction to her. Not that she isn't a lovely woman, as tall as I am with long blonde hair, but I'm not going to lose control and jump her. Even if I *did* feel an attraction to her once upon a time, that's not true now.

I can't look at any woman anymore. All I do, when I see a woman who's beautiful, is just think about Rose and how much more I want her. How badly I wish I was with her. I open up the calendar alert and smirk. Finally. *Finally,* we're free. Rose's professional dreams are going to come true, and we're going to be together. At last, I'll have something to make me happy in life.

I had forgotten what happiness felt like, doing crazy things like renovating my house in an attempt to find it again while stuck in my job that I hate. But Rose has finally given it to me. She's given me that happiness again. And I have no intention of letting her, or that joy, go.

I know she must still be sick, but I text her anyway to let her know. *Today's the day! You're officially unemployed by the company!*

I don't hear anything in response. At first, I think she's sicker than we thought and still recovering. But I don't hear a single damn thing for days. I try texting again. Calling, even. It always goes to voicemail.

Hey, I don't mean to hover or anything, I just want to

make sure you're okay. Are you in the hospital? Hey, it's me again, sorry to be a pain but I'm just worried. Just let me know you're all right.

Nothing.

I decide to call payroll and see if I can get Rose's last check from them, that way I have an excuse to stop by the house and see her. If she's really ill then I want to know about it. I'm not going to run away just because she's got something serious. I would never do that to her. I understand why she might not want to drag me into it if she really is sick, with an early stage of cancer or any other number of things that can hit unexpectedly, even when you're young and generally healthy.

I'm not going anywhere. I want to stick this out. I'm not the kind of person who's going to love someone and then turn and run the second it gets difficult. I want Rose, and I'm not going to give her up, or the joy and life she brings me, so easily. *It's probably fine,* I tell myself. I'm just spinning out into thinking about the worst-case scenarios because of Dad. It's fine. It's probably all fine. Rose is fine.

Then payroll gets back to me, informing me that Rose already picked up her check from payroll and took care of her paperwork. That floors me. Rose was here? She stopped by to get everything taken care of and she didn't see me? Didn't reply to any of my calls or texts?

What the fuck is going on?

If she's well enough to stop by the office then she's feeling well enough to be out and about in the world. She's avoiding me. But why? That's it. I decide to stop by the house after work, and I'm not going to leave this time, not until Rose agrees to see me. I don't even stop by my house first. I just pull right up into Chloe's driveway.

I knock on the door for a lot longer this time. I can see a car in the driveway, so I know that Chloe or Rose is home, at least one of them if not both. Finally, right when I'm about to start yelling, the door opens.

Chloe glares at me. "Yes? Did you want something?"

I glare right back at her. "I want to see Rose. She hasn't been replying to me."

"Maybe she doesn't want to reply to you, have you thought about that?"

"At least let me see her. If I fucked up somehow then I want to talk it out. I can't fix it if I don't know what I did wrong."

Chloe frowns at me. "Well. Guess you'll just have to keep wondering, won't you?"

"What do you mean? Let me see her."

"I can't do that."

"And why the fuck not?" I snarl. I'm losing patience pretty damn fast.

"Because," Chloe replies, arching an eyebrow. "She's not here."

"What?" That doesn't make sense. It doesn't compute in my head.

"Rose isn't here. She's gone. She left. And she's not coming back."

"She moved out?" The words feel weird in my mouth.

Chloe nods. "Yup." She pops the "p" like she's chewing bubble gum.

"Where is she?"

Chloe shrugs. "How should I know?"

"You're her cousin, don't you care?"

"Look, she didn't tell me, okay? So I didn't ask. Unlike you, I respect Rose's privacy. So buzz off, okay? She's not here. You can come through the house if you want and take a look if you don't believe me, but she's gone."

It could be a bluff, but I doubt it. What reason would Chloe have to lie to me? Chloe closes the door on me without another word, and I'm left standing on the steps in shock.

Rose is gone. She's vanished.

Chapter 27

Rose

When I realize I'm pregnant, I cry for a long time. I just curl up on the bed and sob, letting it all out. Chloe thinks I'm sick; so she's leaving me alone all day, which means luckily nobody can interrupt me while I cry myself dry. Maybe my family was right all along. Maybe I really am unlucky. Cursed in some way.

I want to be a mother, but not right now. And Simon...

Simon told his mother that he didn't want children. When I talked to him afterward, he admitted he was sorry for being so harsh with her, but he never said that he did actually want to be a father. He meant what he said. He just didn't mean for it to come out like that, so angry and hurtful.

I can't go to him with this. Simon has tied himself to a job he hated just because he knew it was his father's wish. I know exactly how he'll handle this. He'll offer to marry me and take care of the child, even though he doesn't want to. I'm sure our child will want nothing physically and financially. But would that really matter when Simon's heart wouldn't be in it?

I love him. I *love* him. I can't trap him in another life he doesn't want, and after his work life has become something he hates. I can't make him as unhappy at home as he is at his job. And while theoretically you can sell a company or give the job to someone else, once you have a child, you can't walk out on them, not really. A child is forever. Simon wouldn't ever be able to undo being a father, I couldn't ever undo giving him that child.

It wouldn't be fair to the child, either, if I were to give them a father who didn't really want them. I'm sure the kid would feel it.

Long before I told my parents I was going to move out west and try my hand at having a fashion label, I knew they wouldn't approve. If I did anything that they didn't feel was "sensible", they'd dismiss me. You don't need something to be said out loud to understand it and become aware of it, even as a child.

I'll never do that to my kid. Never.

That means I can't tell Simon. I can't let him know. I didn't plan to be a mother right now, but I don't know when I'll get the chance again. If I can't have kids with Simon... then I don't know that I ever will.

It was something I was putting off thinking about and letting it just sit in the back of my mind. I know, smart, right? And now it's come up to slap me in the face. But I can't trust that I'll find someone else that I fall in love with the way I fell for Simon. Balancing both a kid and starting a business will be hard. It'll be the hardest thing I've ever done. But if I want to be a mother, I don't know when the universe will provide me with another opportunity.

Now I just have to figure out what to tell my family.

I'm in bed for so long, just curled up there, that the shadows get long across the floor and eventually the door opens.

"Hey, you okay?" Chloe steps inside. "Oh. You... have you moved at all?"

I shake my head.

The tear stains on my face must be obvious as Chloe comes closer and sits next to me on the bed. "Hey, what's wrong, huh? Talk to me."

She strokes my hair. I don't know the last time my cousin's ever been so gentle and sweet... and not saccharine the way she gets with her girlfriends—that fake, cloying "niceness" that feels so shallow—it's genuine, loving sweetness.

I must really look more of a mess than I thought.

"Bathroom," I croak.

Chloe frowns, and then gets up and goes into the bathroom. A moment later I hear her inhale sharply, and I know she's seen the two tests sitting on the counter.

She returns and sits next to me. Resumes stroking my hair. "What are you going to do?"

"Keep it."

Chloe nods. "Okay."

We sit there in silence for a while. Well, I lie there. Chloe sits and pets my hair.

"Is the father the guy you were telling me about?"

I nod. "I overheard him say once to his mother that he doesn't want kids. So..."

Chloe exhales loudly. "Okay. So will he get mad or refuse to pay child support or...?"

I sit up. "No, I can't tell him. He'll try to do the right thing and he'll make all of us miserable in the process. He works for his father's company although he's always hated it because his father wanted it, and he thinks it's the right thing to do. He'd make himself miserable all over again by marrying me and being a father. I can't do that to him."

I also can't watch the connection we've shared, the love that's growing between us, wilt and rot because of our child —because we're married out of obligation. I can't have that happen between us. It'll kill me.

I'd rather lose Simon now and leave him, with the memory of how good things were between us, than watch that good thing sour.

"You need child support, though. You're starting a company, Rose, you can't do this all on your own."

"I'll do it anyway." I wipe at my eyes, my stomach settling with determination. "I'm not going to give up on my dream. If I'm successful, I can set my own hours. I'll be able to spend time with my kid in a way working in an office wouldn't let me."

Chloe frowns, looking dubious. I can already imagine what she's going to say. She's about to tell me that this is a stupid idea and I need to go home to my parents and work for my dad—to give up my dream and let my family help me raise the kid. She's going to make a quip about my bad luck and how it's just like me to have something like this happen.

"Well then." Chloe takes my hand. "I guess that I'm just gonna have to make sure that, as your investor, you're getting all the help you need to make this a success."

I gape at her. "What?"

Chloe smiles, small and tentative. "You were right, before, when you said that we needed to support you better. I'm not great at... well. I don't have a lot of practice. But I have lots of money to spare. I want to help you. So whatever you need... we'll get you an apartment and buy you baby supplies. We'll do as much damn work together as we can so that by the time you have your kid, your business is up and running. We have about nine months, right? That's a lot of time. We can get plenty done."

My eyes water again and I sniffle. "Chloe..."

I have nothing to say. I hug her tightly. She wraps her arms around me in return. "I want to be here for you, Rose."

"You are." I sob into her shoulder. "Thank you. This means... I don't have words."

She rubs my back. "We're gonna get through this together. You're my cousin. You're family. We're here for each other."

I nod in agreement.

Chloe's always been spoiled. Maybe this wouldn't be so surprising coming from someone else, but to have Chloe thinking about me and promising to support me—to give me whatever I need—she's thinking about someone other than herself for the first time since I've known her. She's choosing that someone to be me. She loves me.

It's not the same as Simon, but it does help me to feel loved and supported.

At last, we pull back. "Are you sure you don't want to tell him?"

I shake my head. "It's—it's complicated. It's been complicated."

"There's stuff you aren't telling me."

I sigh. "Simon isn't just your next-door neighbor. He's also my boss. Or he was my boss. I put in my two weeks so that we can be together."

Chloe's eyebrows shoot up.

"You can't tell anyone!" I blurt out.

"I won't, Jeez, I know how much trouble you could get in. Or he could get in, probably. That's like, an abuse of power, right? Because he's your boss?"

"Yes, there's a power dynamic at play. While I might have gotten in trouble, most of it would fall on Simon." I pause. "Maybe not in most cases, unfortunately, since he's the CEO and could probably do whatever he wanted if he felt like it. But Simon's the kind of guy who would take whatever punishment came for him."

"He sounds like a really good guy." Chloe's voice sounds small and sad, as if she realizes just what I'm now losing.

I nod. "He is." I wipe at my eyes, sick of crying and yet unable to stop. "He really is."

"So that's why you've been so cagey about him."

"Yeah. The plan was that... well, we didn't know when we first started our... thing. And then when we found out, we tried to just keep away from each other until I had my business underway enough to quit. When you offered to be my investor, I put in my two weeks so I could focus on my business, and we could be together. But now..."

Chloe sighs. "You're sure you don't want to tell him?"

"I won't burden him. I'm sure."

That means I have to leave. I have to move out and disappear. Change my number and make sure that Simon can't find me. He says he loves me; it's not that I don't believe him, but I'm also sure that he'll find a way to move on from me. It's going to be okay. *He's* going to be okay.

Most importantly, he's going to be free.

"But wouldn't he want to know the truth?" Chloe asks. "So he can make an informed decision?"

"You don't know him. He'll do what he feels he should do, not what he actually wants to do. No matter how miserable it makes him." I take Chloe's hands in mine. "You can't tell him. If he comes looking for me. You can't tell him, you can't tell anyone. Okay? I'll tell my parents it was just a one-night stand, they have no reason to believe otherwise. Nobody knows that I've had any kind of relationship. Please, Chloe. You have to promise me."

Chloe doesn't look happy about it, but she nods. "I promise."

Now there's nothing more to do than... well, disappear. I go in and change my phone number, then delete myself off the NextDoor app and everything else that Simon knows about. I pick up my last paycheck and handle the HR stuff for quitting without telling Simon I'm there—just going to the office, knowing he's a few floors up, so close and yet so far, is torture, but I make it through.

Chloe and I shop around for apartments. I don't want to make her spend too much money since she'll be footing the bill, but she insists on helping me find a nice place, and we settle on something in West Hollywood. It's not too far from Bel Air so Chloe can visit easily. It's in a fun and vibrant neighborhood with a large park and a library nearby that'll be fun to take my child when they're old enough.

All told, it only takes a few days for me to erase myself from Simon's life so he can't find me. I'm sure if he was really determined he could hire a hacker or something, but I know him. He's an honorable man. He won't go that far. Now all I can do is pray that he forgives me for leaving him. All I can do is hope that, somehow, he has a happy life without me.

Chapter 28

Simon

I 've never had my heart broken before. Oh, sure, when I was fourteen and my crush started dating someone else I thought I was heartbroken. It feels so big and deep when you're a teenager. Everything does. But as I grew up, my attention was completely on my career, and then my father's legacy. I had a lot of sex, but I was never, for one moment, under the impression that I was in love. Romance was just... not even in the equation.

Now it feels like someone's carved a hole in my organs, and I'm walking around bleeding all day, every day, it's just that no one can see it.

Rose's cousin is adamant that Rose is gone, and she doesn't know where Rose went. "She wouldn't tell me," Chloe keeps repeating.

Finally, I just stop asking. I'm not sure if I believe Chloe or not. On the one hand, she's Rose's damn cousin, how could she not have asked Rose where she's going or found out her plans? On the other hand, Rose had mentioned multiple times how Chloe is self-focused and a bit of an airhead. She could very well not know jack shit because

Rose didn't trust her. Or hell, maybe Rose did fucking tell her and Chloe forgot because Rose's family doesn't have a good track record with actually paying attention to what she needs and wants.

It makes me so angry. I could take care of Rose. I could give her all the support and love she deserves. I don't understand what happened. I'm not angry at Rose. I'm sure that whatever it was, she has a good reason. It just feels like I'm cycling through the stages of grief, from denial to anger to bargaining to depression—just never hitting on "acceptance".

Chloe won't give me any information, though; it's a bust when I discreetly ask around the office. I even ask N, just in case Rose called her and asked for a reference at a new job or something since they seemed to be friendly and Rose would text N with questions sometimes.

But N hasn't heard anything. "Are you okay? You sound frantic."

"I'm fine," I lie, and then I hang up before she can interrogate me further.

I just wish I could understand. For a couple of weeks, I mope. I'm man enough to admit it. I definitely mope. I come into the office as little as possible and just do the bare minimum. I have no energy. I just feel like I'm in constant pain, somewhere deep inside.

The thing is that... it isn't just that I'm in love with Rose. It's that she's the person who brought happiness to my life. I had forgotten what that really felt like until Rose came along—being happy. Now that I've remembered what that feels like, I don't want to lose it.

My heartbreak slowly calcifies into determination. If I can't have Rose—if she's really gone—I should do what she urged me to do so gently. Rose isn't always a gentle person, but she's kind and she was gentle with me about this. She wanted me to be happy and pursue my dreams of being a chef… to let go of the idea that I had to spend the rest of my life honoring my father's legacy.

She thought that if my father loved me, as I believe he did, then he would want me to be happy above all. Maybe it's time to find that out.

Mom's heartbroken in her own way when I tell her that the "thing" with my girl didn't work out. "I don't really want to talk about it," I admit, and for once, Mom listens and doesn't press the issue. I think she can tell how much I'm hurting.

She puts up a lot more of a fuss about the company. In a way, it's a relief to have it out in the open, and it sure as hell distracts from the issue of Rose.

"Your father wanted you to take over. He always has."

"I know. And I did my time with the company. I worked on it for years even though it's making me miserable. But Dad was a good man, and he loved me. You're always remembering how he loved me. If he did, then wouldn't he want me to be happy? I've got the company in a good place. I'll find someone who really cares to take it over. Shouldn't it be someone who enjoys the work to be in charge? Rather than someone who resents it?"

Mom ponders that. I sigh and lean back in my chair. I invited her over so I could cook for her; neither of us would feel embarrassed for being out in public if the conversation got heated.

"Look, you want to know the truth?"

Mom nods. "Of course I do, sweetheart."

"Rose isn't just the cousin of my next-door neighbor. She was also my assistant."

Mom frowns. "Rose…" Her eyes go wide. "I met her!"

"Yeah. When we had our fight."

"Your *assistant*? Simon..."

"I know, I know, but we met before she was hired. I put Nadia in charge of hiring my new assistant. I didn't want to be in the office. I figured she'd do a better job of it than I would since she'd pick someone who could actually handle me and stand up to me the way Nadia does. It wasn't until afterward..."

"And you two decided to keep dating?" Mom sounds scandalized, and I can't blame her.

"No. We decided to wait until Rose could get a different job or get her personal business off the ground. She'd put in her two weeks when she vanished."

"Vanished?"

"Yes. Dropped off the face of the damn earth."

"Well, honey you know there are ways you can..."

"You want me to stalk her like that? No. If Rose doesn't want to be found... if she's changed her number and didn't tell her cousin where she's going—or the cousin won't tell me—then I'm not going to violate her wishes by hiring a fucking private detective or something."

"But if something went wrong—"

"I don't know why she left, okay? I don't know. I wish I did but I don't. But I do know if something was really wrong, her cousin wouldn't have acted the way she did. Chloe's shallow, but I never got the impression she was callous or that she didn't care about Rose."

I take several deep breaths to calm down and lean forward on my elbows. "Mom, what I'm trying to say here is that if I hadn't had this job, Rose and I never would've had to wait to get together. We still could've met, and we could've started dating right away. I know, it was just a bad coincidence, but this is the second thing that this job has taken from me that I love."

Mom looks at me for a long moment, her eyes soft. "You really love her that much? You really love cooking that much?"

"Yes, and yes."

Mom looks away. "I suppose I thought... your father had his hobbies. So do I. We all do. You know at one point I really wanted to be in musical theater?"

"No, I had no idea."

She looks back at me and smiles, the twist of her mouth bittersweet. "It wasn't meant to be, and I don't regret it. But at one time I really wanted it. I thought... we all have dreams. And we let them go and we move on. I thought that yours were like that."

I shake my head. "I've wanted it every single day. I've hated going into that damn office every single day."

Mom looks like she might cry. She won't because she's too dignified for that, no matter how much she likes to wail at me. "You're... determined, aren't you?"

I think about it for a long moment. All this time I've felt tied to my father's legacy. I haven't wanted to hurt his memory or my mother by abandoning the company that meant so much to him. I wasn't sure if I could live with myself if the people who took over after I left ran the place into the ground.

I just lost out, once again, on something that would give me joy because of this job. I don't know how many times I'm supposed to let that happen before I snap.

"I forgot what it was like to be happy. Rose reminded me. And now that I've had it... I know it's because of my job that I lost it... so yeah, I'm determined. I can't do this anymore, Mom, I can't. And I know that we can't say for sure what Dad would think if he was alive. But I know how much he loved you and believed in your relationship. I think he'd want me to have that for myself. I hope that if he saw how miserable I really was... he'd be okay with me passing the company along to someone else."

Mom presses her lips together and nods, looking at a point over my shoulder. Finally, she drags her eyes back to my face. "It's hard to say what your father would feel. For one thing, I think if he lived..." She sighs. "I think he would only just now be considering retirement. I know he didn't intend for you to take over for a while. So I... I wonder if he would've been stubborn."

"I would've had years to run my own restaurant at that point so it would've been a different conversation," I reply, thinking out loud.

Mom nods.

"We can't know what he would want. But he loved me, right?"

Mom nods again, her face softening. "Of course he did, sweetheart. He loved you so very much. It was never a question. He thought you would enjoy running the company like he did and that's part of why he wanted it. He wanted you to have the life that he did."

I take her hand. "I know. But you understand I have to do this, right? I have to let this go. We have to let *Dad* go. He's gone and all we can do now... all I can do... is what makes me happy. I don't know why Rose left. But I do know that I love her; she might not have left if I'd been able to be with her this whole time."

Mom looks heartbroken. "Honey..."

I pull my hand back. I don't want pity and sympathy, even from Mom. "I don't—what's done is done. But Rose wanted me to quit; she wanted me to be happy. I can do that. I can't have her, but I can have something else. And I'm going to do it."

Mom sighs and sits back in her chair. "I want you to be happy, honey, and if this is what it's time to do..." She sighs again and tucks her hair behind her ear. "Maybe you're right. Maybe it is time we let him go."

I can't live in my father's shadow anymore. I have to do what makes me happy. I hope that, wherever she is, Rose is proud of me. I start the next day.

Finding and training a successor takes a few months. I'm not going to give over control of my father's company to just anyone, no matter how badly I want to quit and just get out of here. My father, the company he built, all the people who've put care and dedication into it, and the employees who rely on me for their livelihood, all deserve better than that.

Eventually, I settle on someone who isn't a junior executive or isn't a member of the board. I don't pick someone who has experience owning another company.

I pick the person who knows more about the company than anyone else because she's spent all of her time managing me, someone who I turn to for advice, someone who practically ran the place because I didn't really want to.

I pick Nadia.

She needs some additional training of course. But I realize she's the only person I trust to take care of the company the right way once I'm gone. She knows the company inside and out from working for me all this time. If she can handle me, then she can definitely handle any spoiled brats or stuck-up assholes.

Nadia's shocked when I offer her the job, but she's happy about it. "I just never thought that I'd get that kind of offer. It's not really how it works when you work at a company. Assistants stay assistants until they move somewhere else and get a managerial role."

"Well, I don't really work like most people do."

I'm trying for a joke, but Nadia gives me a sharp look. I haven't talked to her about Rose. I think she suspects something, anyway. Nadia's my best friend. She knows when something's up, even if I don't tell her about it. I can't tell her about it. It hurt enough to tell Mom. I don't want to open myself back up like that again and pick at the wound.

Once Nadia is finally settled into her new position, I'm able to officially step down as CEO and hand her the reins. Oh, yeah, there's some hearty protesting. Mostly from the board and some other stuffed shirts who are mad that they weren't chosen to replace me instead or think that an assistant can't possibly do a good job.

Dad built this company up from nothing. I know that Nadia can do just as good of a job as he did. Once I get everything taken care of and set up, I don't feel the sense of freedom I expected. I feel... a bit scared, actually.

I think about Rose, and how she must be feeling. While I no longer am quite as rich as I was when I was CEO, and I don't have access to the same kind of assets, I still have billions of dollars at my disposal. I can let my restaurant fail —hell, I can fail a dozen restaurants—and I'll be fine.

Rose doesn't have that kind of cushion, even with her cousin supporting her, if that's even still happening. For her sake, for her bravery and her gumption, I need to do the same. She wanted me to go after the life that I truly wanted. I owe her that much. I owe *myself* that much.

I start putting together a plan. I don't want to do anything too fucking pretentious, so I abandon the Westside and Beverly Hills immediately. I pick something downtown, something fun and boundary-pushing. I have a love for all kinds of different foods, so it's a struggle to narrow it down. Eventually, I decide on a tavern-style restaurant with a fusion of classic American food and more international flavors, like a tikka masala burger and soy egg fries. It's fun, adventurous, and unpretentious with large portions and experimentation.

I like to think Rose would be proud of me.

I name the place *Hedgeclimber*. When people ask, I explain that it's the idea of climbing over your neighbor's hedge, one culture bleeding into another; and the fusion and sharing of ideas that make the United States so great. It's the idea that we can only innovate and push forward in the culinary world—in any world—if we continue to climb over each other's hedges and collaborate. But of course, the truth is that it's named after Rose.

Only she'd know that. I don't plan to ever tell anyone else. If someone ever suspected it would be Chloe or Mom, but I doubt it. I haven't even so much as heard a peep from my next-door neighbor all this time. I have no idea what Chloe's up to, and I haven't wanted to reach out. I have the feeling she'd slam the door in my face, anyway.

That doesn't mean that I don't harbor a stupid hope that someday, maybe, I can track her down. Or—even more unlikely—someday she'll see the restaurant or hear about it and realize that it's named for her. I know it's a stupid hope. But I can't help it. You'd think that after a year and a half without her that the feelings I've had for her would start to fade, but you'd be dead wrong. I still love her and can't get her out of my head.

It's not that I'm not happy. I am, actually. Coming up with recipes and being back in the kitchen, knowing that I'm feeding people and getting to do what I love, has me happier than before. I've actually hired a construction team finally. I don't feel the need to do the construction at my house myself anymore. And if I have them redo the house from the ground up in a more Art Nouveau style, well, nobody has to know.

I do sometimes wonder if I should go to Chloe and try to interrogate her. She has to know something, right? Unless Rose decided to cut off her family. What if that was what happened? Did Chloe decide not to financially support her? Did Rose not know what to do because she'd put in her two weeks with me? Did she feel she had to choose between a rock and a hard place?

These questions keep me up at night, but I manage to resist the urge to look for her and be creepy about it. Someday, hopefully, she'll come back into my life. I have to hope that she meant it when she said she loved me, too. I have to hope that this all means something.

Then *Hedgeclimber* is bought out for a special event. We don't get bought out often since it's so damn expensive. We quickly become one of the most popular and trendiest spots in the city, and I don't want to turn down a full night of reservations for one group.

My hostess assures me that the person was willing to pay top dollar. It's a lunch event on a weekday; that minimizes the loss of reservations. It's to celebrate the successful launch of a company, apparently, and the entrepreneur is the guest of honor.

Well, good for them. I work out a menu and let my events manager handle everything else. I can step in as a manager when I need to, but I'm not a CEO anymore for a reason, damn it. I like to focus on the food.

Of course, I'm on-site for the date of the event, making the food. When I hear the guests start to arrive and enter the restaurant, I finish the food and change into a clean apron. It's important for me to greet the guests, so they get the face behind the food.

There's a tall woman with a blonde bob who seems to be in charge of the whole thing. I walk over to her and introduce myself as the owner and head chef.

"Oh my God, we're so glad that you had availability!" She shakes my hand with enthusiasm. "I'm Bella, I'm the person who set this all up. We're so excited that we could host the party here. I've eaten here three times already and your food is just *divine*."

"Uh-huh." I grin. It's crazy how, now that I'm a chef at a restaurant, rich people talk to me differently. They don't realize I'm one of them.

I prefer it that way. But it does crack me up to know that this woman, Bella, has no idea that I'm richer than she is.

"I'm sure that everyone will love it here," Bella continues gushing.

"And I'm glad to have you all. I'm excited about the menu that I've put together."

Behind me, I hear the sound of the front door opening. Bella's gaze slides over my shoulder to someone beyond, and her eyes light up as she smiles. "Ahh! Here she is, the woman of the hour!"

I turn as Bella goes around me to greet whoever the guest of honor is—and my heart flies into my throat.

There, standing in the doorway... is Rose. And in her arms is a baby.

Chapter 29

Rose

It's been a difficult year and a half. Starting a business is demanding enough, but doing it while pregnant, and then with an infant, is even more difficult. I felt like I didn't really sleep starting around the last trimester. I don't know how I would've done it without Chloe funding me and helping me out. My cousin really showed herself to be a good person this past year. She's been there for me in a way that I didn't expect her to be capable of.

My parents were less enthusiastic when they learned that I was pregnant and determined to stay in Los Angeles. They thought that I should come home and accept their help. No, thank you. I was not going to give up on my dream, especially because the timing was so bad.

I make my own luck, dammit. I am not going to let my family or circumstances or anything else get in my way. Sure, this isn't how I'd like things to go if I could plan them. But I won't let that stop me. I'm going to own my own business, and it's going to thrive, and I'm going to be a good mother.

Even if it means I can't have the man I love.

My parents and I don't really speak for a while after that. I know they don't approve of many of my decisions, like my insistence on staying in LA and my refusal to tell the father. But I hold firm, and by Christmas, I hear from Chloe that they want to reach out, and they're sorry.

It's a start, at least.

Simon's idea to start with social media is a good one, and Chloe helps me by asking some of her affluent friends to give my clothes a try. If they like them, they will show them off on social media, linking back to my account.

Chloe's rich, of course, and her friends tend to be rich and have large social media followings. So, soon I'm getting more orders than I know what to do with. I have to hire a couple of people, train them to help me make the clothes, and we release them in small batches. And I also create an official website.

It does take me about a year to get everything really rolling, but by then, I've got a steady stream of clients and a lot of people who are excited for me. It's time to finally open my brick-and-mortar store. I'm so excited, but the only thing more exciting was the birth of my child.

It's a boy. I name him after Simon's father, David. I don't recall Simon ever telling me his father's name, but it was easy enough to find out by looking up their company and reading about his father, the founder, on their website.

Simon will never know he has a son; he would want it that way, but if he *did* want a child, he'd want that child to be named after the father he had lost. The whole reason that Simon put up with the job he hated for so long is that he loved his father. If he didn't, I don't think Simon would've wasted a day at that company.

My parents fly out for the birth, excited to meet their first grandchild. I can feel that they're still judging me for not telling the father (and not telling them a thing about Simon), plus for refusing to move in with them and let them help with the baby. But I'm forging my own path, and they keep their thoughts to themselves. Maybe, in time, they'll come around enough to be proud of me. But they worry about me and they love me, and that's a start.

David is a handful, that's for sure. Chloe's terrible with babies and kids, so I try not to ask her for help a lot. She really throws herself into helping me at the company instead. I don't think I've ever seen her so happy, honestly. I think that what she was searching for in a man or in shopping trips was really a sense of fulfillment. Now she has it.

I wish I could say the same.

It's not that being a mother doesn't make me happy. It does. I adore David. The moment he was put into my arms at the hospital I burst into tears because I had no idea that you could love something so much. It was like my heart burst, shattered, and melted because there was no way that I could feel this much love and survive it. David is my whole world. I adore him.

My company gives me the fulfillment I had always hoped for. My dream is coming true. How can I not be happy about that? Chloe says that I'll get over Simon and that it's going to be okay. I just need time, and I'll move on. But my entire pregnancy passes, and all I can do the entire time is think about how much I wish I could tell Simon. The first time David kicked inside me, I wanted Simon there so I could put his hand over my belly and help him feel it.

When I gave birth, I wished it was Simon's hand I was holding instead of my mother's. I wished I could call Simon into the room so that he could hold his child with me. And now, as I prepare to launch my store and celebrate, I wish Simon could be here at my side.

David grows so quickly. He's only six months old, but at the same time, he's already grown a lot. I want Simon to be here to see him. I know Simon would be proud of my accomplishments. I just wish he'd want to be a father as well.

A year and a half later, and I still haven't gotten over how in love with him I am. Maybe I never will. Maybe I won't ever feel completely fulfilled like others in life are. Maybe there will always be that piece of happiness missing for me. I guess I'll have to learn to live with it.

Bella is one of Chloe's friends, and since Chloe introduced us, she's become a friend and a repeat client. She insists on hosting a party for me to celebrate the launch of my store; something classy and small. We can invite some loyal customers and friends, and give it a VIP feeling. I was going to just host something small at the store itself, but Bella wants us to have it at a proper restaurant and suggests this place downtown that's been getting rave reviews. It's called *Hedgeclimber*. My mouth twists in a bittersweet smile as I get out of the car and see the sign.

I don't know why the restaurant is named this, but it makes me think of Simon. How I climbed over his hedges because I was that determined and angry. It's wild to me, still, how someone who had pissed me off so damn much could become someone who means the world to me. And he'll never really know.

I get David out of the car and carry him in my arms into the restaurant. It's a lovely place, with a homey, cozy tavern feel and some nice touches like wood carvings in the ceiling and crown molding. It's not pretentious, which I appreciate, but I still get the feeling that this is a high-end place when I step inside.

Honestly... and maybe this is just the name of the restaurant making me think about him... but I feel like this is the kind of place Simon would like. It reminds me of the rustic style he was doing his house over in, but natural touches remind me of the Art Nouveau movement. One of its goals was to incorporate emblems of nature into the interior design—to bring some of the outdoors indoors.

Almost like a marriage of our two styles.

I shake my head, trying to banish the thought. I can't afford to think about Simon right now. I just hope that wherever he is, he's happy.

"Rose!" Bella calls, and I look over to see her heading toward me with a smile. "I was just speaking to the head chef, I'm so excited that we could secure a spot here, you must meet him..."

The man himself steps forward. I can feel my jaw drop and my eyes go wide. To his credit, he looks just as shocked as I feel.

It's Simon.

"Rose." Simon's voice is a little rough. "Bella was just telling me you're the guest of honor."

I nod, dumbfounded. Simon's gaze drifts to David in my arms, and I feel a lump forming in my throat. How am I supposed to tell him the truth? But how am I supposed to lie to him?

"Simon here makes such delicious food," Bella chatters on, completely unaware of the emotions going on in front of her. I like Bella, but she is kind of like Chloe in that way, a bit oblivious to the things that aren't about her. "And he's so charming and handsome."

Bella simpers at him, clearly hoping that she'll get a chance to flirt, but Simon's gaze stays locked on mine.

"I hope that you enjoy the food," he tells me.

"Thank you. You... you own this place?"

"Yes. I started it about... a little over half a year ago."

"Half a year."

"It took time to train my successor at my old job. My assistant, actually. She's doing a remarkable job in my place."

Nadia. He must mean Nadia. I didn't know the woman super well, but from what I did know of her, she was fantastic. No-nonsense, capable, kind, but firm... and she had to manage Simon and his reluctance to be in charge all that time. I have no doubt she knew the company inside and out.

"That's amazing." I mean it, although I try not to gush too hard. I don't want Bella finding out that we know one another. I have the feeling Simon's in agreement with me on that since he hasn't given an indication that he knows me. "Good for her."

"I'm very proud of her." Simon smiles. "But, please, let your adoring crowd give you the attention you deserve. I'm just here to provide the food."

"Oh, I'm sure you do so much more than that," Bella says, practically batting her lashes.

I roll my eyes once I'm sure she can't see me, and I see Simon's jaw go tense as he struggles not to laugh. For a second, it's natural between us again—the two of us being sassy together— everything else melting away.

Bella grabs me by the wrist and tugs on me. "Ah, everyone else is arriving!"

The moment is broken.

Simon pulls away and heads back toward the kitchen,

and I'm pulled into the crowd with my friends and admirers. It's nice, of course it is, to get such positive attention. But it also makes me feel sick, because all I want to do is hurry after Simon and talk to him. I want to ask him how he's doing, and how the hell he ended up leaving the company he was so determined to suffer through, leading to owning a restaurant.

This was his dream, and I'm so glad he's achieved it. I just have questions. But he must also have questions for me. I saw how he stared at David. God, what does he think of me? Does he think I'm with someone else? Babies' ages are hard to tell when they're so young. I'm sure he can see that David isn't a newborn anymore but beyond that...

I swallow it all down and focus on my girlfriends who have come here to support me.

The food really is amazing, and with every bite, I want to turn to Simon and tell him how much I love it, but I don't see him the entire party. He stays in the kitchen, and I can't get away from the others for long enough to go back there and talk to him.

I'm not even sure I want to. I do, but I'm also terrified. I have no idea what he'll say or how it'll go. I abandoned him with no explanation. He has every right to hate me.

At last, the party starts winding down, and Simon comes out again to help clean up and accept compliments from my other guests. I pass David off to one of my girlfriends, *not* Chloe since I know she'll be freaking out internally the entire time.

Bella's trying to flirt with him again, but Simon ducks around her, takes some empty plates, and sees me staring at him. He jerks his head towards the kitchen. I nod, and when he heads that way, I wait a moment and then follow. Luckily the kitchen entrance is by the restrooms, so nobody should notice where I'm really going.

The moment we're back there, I see a couple of other people hard at work cleaning up, but Simon just sets the plates down and takes me by the hand to lead me through the kitchen and into what seems to be the manager's office. He closes the door. This close to him, it's so hard to resist flinging my arms around him. Seeing him, hearing his voice... hell, *smelling* him this close-up and getting a whiff of his cologne, has me going crazy.

I missed him. I missed him so fucking much.

"Rose." Simon opens his mouth, closes it, then clears his throat. "How are you doing?"

I almost burst out into hysterical laughter. It seems that neither of us really knows what to say. I almost want to default to arguing with him, just so we're back on familiar ground; but I don't want to upset him or genuinely hurt his feelings, either. "I'm... okay. It's been busy."

"You seem successful. I'm glad."

"Thank you. You left the company."

"I did." Simon blows out a breath. "It's because of you."

My heart races. "Me?"

"You made me happy. You reminded me what happiness even was. I know you wanted me to quit and leave, and do what I wanted with my life. When you left I—I couldn't have you, and our happiness, anymore. I realized I was sick of not being happy. So I decided to seize what happiness I could in another way." Simon pauses. "I imagined that you would be proud of me."

"I am proud of you." I want to reach out and touch him so badly, but I hold back. "I'm so proud of you, Simon, really. And... are you, happy?"

"Mostly." He gives me a small, bittersweet smile. "I'm happy that I get to do what I love now. Getting out of the office and back into the kitchen is... it's amazing. Thank you for encouraging me... for being the reason I did it."

"Of course. Thank you for believing in me. I don't know if I would've had the courage to talk to Chloe or... or keep going, without you."

Simon's smile grows a little, but it's still bittersweet. "So. Uh. The kid."

My stomach twists. I should have known he would ask about that. "Yes. The baby. David."

"David?"

I nod. I can't lie to him. Even if he's unhappy, even if he's angry... I can't lie to him.

Tears well up in my eyes. "I. I wanted to name him after your father."

"My father?"

"Because... well. I thought that's what you would want. If you wanted a child." I shrug helplessly, the tears spilling over and sliding down my cheeks. "He's yours, after all."

Simon looks absolutely shocked for the first time in his life. "Wh—why—you never—mine?"

His voice sounds so soft in my ears. Soft and almost lost.

"Yes. He's yours. I—I knew you didn't want kids. After that fight with your mother, I knew... so I didn't say anything. I would never take advantage of you for child support."

"Is that why you left?" Simon frowns. "Because you thought I wouldn't want to be a father?"

"Of course it is! Did you think I didn't love you?"

"I didn't know what to think. Just that you didn't want to be found."

"I didn't want you to resent me. I didn't want what we had to become this... horrible angry thing. I didn't want our connection to be... rotten... because you were stuck with a kid you didn't want. I wanted to respect your wishes. But, well, I wanted to be a mother; so I decided to keep the baby —to keep David—and just go it alone."

"Without even—Rose, you could've at least asked me for financial support."

"As if you would've done anything less than been a father and married me." I scoff. "You ran your father's company for years while hating it because you loved him, and it was what you wanted. You felt a sense of obligation. Don't tell me for one second that you wouldn't marry a woman you didn't love, or you wouldn't be a father to a child you didn't want, just because you felt it was the right thing to do."

Simon opens his mouth to protest, then closes it and gives me a rueful look. Yeah, he knows that I've got him there.

"I wouldn't be the reason you were unhappy at home as well as at work." I stand by that, even though Simon is currently looking at me as though I've ripped his heart out.

Simon nods and looks away, and I take a deep breath. Here it comes. He'll tell me that he still wants to give me some kind of child support. He's going to awkwardly offer to give me financial assistance. We're going to do a whole song and dance. Or, maybe, he'll tell me that I was right. He'll wish me well, we'll part ways, and we'll never see each other again.

Instead, Simon turns back to look at me with a look of determination on his face—and drops to one knee.

"I know I don't have a ring at the moment. But..." Simon gives me a smile that is, for the first time since I've run into him again, only joy and not pain. "Rose, will you marry me?"

What!?

Chapter 30

Simon

To say I'm shocked that this baby is my kid is... an understatement. It never occurred to me that the kid could be mine. I'm not great at judging the ages of babies, and I know that theoretically the baby could be mine... I just felt like if it was, then Rose would tell me.

I'd completely forgotten about the hurtful things I said to my mother in my anger. And that Rose had overheard it all. Damn, she thought this whole time that I didn't want to be a parent. That wasn't really something on my radar, but what I said to Mom was just... whatever I could think of to say in the moment that would hurt her. I was angry and hurting, and I lashed out.

I thought Rose had understood that. But I didn't really clear it up for her. Why would I have? We weren't even technically supposed to be dating, and while I knew from our first official date that I wanted to marry her, I also didn't think to have any kind of talk with her about things like weddings and kids. We'd already done so many things backward, so why would I rush into that?

When I saw her with the baby stepping into my restaurant, my heart sank. I thought she moved on and had a kid with someone else... the lack of a wedding ring on her finger had reassured me a little, but not much. Rose is an independent woman who started her own business. She could've been in a serious relationship and just decided she wasn't quite ready to get married yet.

The whole time during the party I had to try and stay in the kitchen so I wouldn't watch her like a sad, lovesick puppy. She had to be with someone else; I was sure of it. But I needed to talk to her and find out what had happened.

And she tells me that the baby is mine.

Not only is the baby mine, but she's named him after my father. It's exactly what I would've done if I'd had a say in it. I would have asked her: if the baby is a boy, could we name him David—Rose somehow knew. She understood and she went and named him after the man I loved, looked up to, and lost; even though she thought I wouldn't want to be in our baby's life.

It makes my heart break all over again—but it also fills me with joy because it means that Rose hasn't moved on. She can still be mine. I'm upset that I missed her pregnancy and couldn't be there to take care of and support her. She had to be a single mother and start a business without me, and it hurts like someone's pried my chest open. But that's okay. I'll make it okay because I'm not going to waste another second of my life without her.

Rose and I have found happiness in our professional lives—I have my restaurant and she has her fashion business. Now it's time we find happiness in our personal lives, too. I love her. I've loved her this whole time. Especially with baby David in the picture, I don't particularly feel like waiting or going slow.

I drop to one knee. "I know I don't have a ring at the

moment." Something I'm going to rectify as soon as possible. "But... Rose, will you marry me?"

Rose gapes at me. "What!?"

"You heard me."

"Have you lost your mind?"

I grin. "No, just my heart."

"Oh my God." Rose's face goes pink as she blushes. "That's the corniest thing I've ever heard."

"But you liked it."

"I..." Rose wipes at her eyes. "Maybe." She shakes it off. "But you can't really mean that. Simon, I won't let you tie yourself to me out of a sense of obligation."

"It's not obligation. It's the fact that I'm in love with you." I stand up and take her hands. "I've missed you this entire time. I want to be with you, and I want to be a father to our child."

"You said you didn't want children." Rose's voice is soft and surprised.

"I was trying to spite my mother. I was angry with how my parents had controlled the course of my life, even if it was through good intentions. I knew she wanted me to give her grandkids, so I said whatever I thought would hurt her. But I'm done living my life according to what my parents want. That doesn't just mean I'm not going to do what they want—it means I'm not going to *not* do something, just to spite them. I'm going to do whatever I want. And if that happens to include something my mom also wants, well, lucky her I guess."

Rose stares at me for a moment, her eyes brimming with tears again. "You... you really want this? You want me? You want our child?"

I take her face in my hands. "Of course I do. That's all I've wanted this whole time."

I can taste the salt from her tears when she kisses me, but that's all right. I'm going to fix it. I'm going to make sure that she never doubts my love for her ever again.

"Can I meet him?" I murmur. "Our son?"

Rose nods, still crying. "Yes. Yes, of course."

Pretty much everyone has left the party by the time we get back into the restaurant. Chloe is sitting with baby David. I'm pretty sure that she isn't pleased, given that she looks like someone handed her a live grenade and told her to babysit it.

Rose takes David from her cousin and brings him over to me. "David," she coos, "meet your father, Simon."

She gently helps me take the baby—*my son*—into my arms, nestling his head in the crook of my elbow. Tears spring into my eyes. This is my son. My baby boy. He stares up at me with big, familiar eyes, eyes that remind me of his mother. I feel like he just swallowed my heart and will keep it inside of him now. I stroke his soft downy head.

"I'm going to take care of you from now on," I promise him in a murmur.

I look up and see Rose staring at us. I pull her in and kiss her. "Both of you. I'm giving you a big damn wedding, Rose Faraday, and you can't stop me."

I can't wait to show her the house. I'm sure we can turn one of the spare rooms into a beautiful nursery.

At last, after everything... I have the job I love, and the woman I love. I'm even a father. After all these years of living for the ghost of someone else, I'm living for myself.

And I'm happy.

Epilogue

Rose

We want to get married as soon as possible.

Even when you're not planning a fancy wedding, it still takes time to plan, and so we do have to wait a few months. If we went to the courthouse, I think Simon's mother and my parents would band together and kill us both for it, but Simon and I still want something low-key.

We plan everything together. We're having the reception at our place, in the home that Simon remodeled just for me, even though he knew I might never see any of it. I still can't quite believe that he would do something like that for me; that anyone could be so in love with me; and that they'd want to make a home I would love, just for the sake of my memory and as a way to keep me close.

I hope that I show him, every day, just how much I love him in return.

Because we're planning everything together and keeping it small and simple, there aren't very many surprises on the big day. My parents, to my surprise, adore Simon.

I'd honestly been a little worried. My parents are so bad at supporting whatever it is I want in life that I figured just by virtue of wanting to be with Simon, fate would dictate that he be the kind of guy my parents didn't want for me. But there is one thing you can say about my parents: they would never dream of me marrying someone for their money. They know I'm far too proud for that kind of thing.

And they do like him. They like him a lot. And they adore their grandson, so that helps.

Finally, the day comes, and I wake up about to get married. And there is *one* surprise that I've managed to preserve:

The dress.

I haven't let Simon see it or hear anything about it. He knows I got one, obviously, but he doesn't know anything about the design itself. I wanted it to be a surprise for him when he sees me coming down the aisle.

I immediately knew what I was going to do for my wedding dress. I was going to design it myself, and I was going to base it off of some Waterhouse paintings. I did everything on my own, just buying materials, and then stayed up late sewing it in the workshop above my store. I sowed it at home, too, in the designated sewing and crafting room that Simon made for me, but I didn't want to risk him coming home and seeing it one day by accident.

Now, it's the big day, and I can't wait.

My father gives me his arm as we prepare to walk down the aisle. My cousin just went, and I can already see her eyeing some of Simon's groomsmen. I fondly roll my eyes. She's going to figure herself out on her own time, or she's not, and either way, it's not my problem.

"Are you ready?" Dad asks me in a whisper.

I nod, smiling. My son is up at the front with Mom and

Simon's mother, and Simon's standing at the front of the altar, waiting for us to officially become a married couple. I've never been so ready in my life.

"I'm proud of you," Dad tells me, and my knees nearly give out.

I never thought I would hear that from him. I gave up on hearing him say that to me years ago. But here I am, with a successful business doing the work I love; with a man who's also doing what he loves; and in the house of our dreams with a beautiful baby boy. My life is everything I could've hoped it to be and more.

And it's made my father finally proud of me.

"Thanks, Dad," I whisper, kissing him on the cheek. I mean it.

The music starts and Dad walks me down the aisle. Simon turns to look at me—and I see the moment he catches me because his face flushes and tears spring into his eyes.

He smiles, like he can't believe that this is actually real and I'm actually in front of him. I smile back, feeling my vision blur as my own eyes get damp.

This is the happiest day of my life. The day we officially become a family.

I walk down the aisle with my father, in my lovely dress, and Simon catches my hands with his as I reach him. "You look amazing," he murmurs. "Exquisite."

He smiles as I walk up and I can feel the fabric of my dress flowing and swishing around me. "You like it?"

"Of course I like it. You're so beautiful."

I want him to kiss me, and I know he wants to, but we both refrain, trying to hold it in until we get through the ceremony.

"How do you feel?" Simon whispers as the officiant reminds everyone that we have an official wedding photographer, so please keep all cell phones put away and on silent. "Nervous?"

"Not at all." I squeeze his hands. "I feel happy. You?"

"Rose," he tells me seriously, "the only day that's better than this one is the day we met."

"The day we argued?"

"The day that you came into my life. This? All of it? My whole life? Is because of you." Simon smiles. "But I suppose today is a close second."

I laugh. The officiant asks Simon and I if we're ready to start, and we begin the ceremony. And I say the words that will make Simon my husband, and me his wife, forever.

Yeah, I see what Simon means, and I think it's romantic and adorable, in Simon's own way. But I have to disagree with him. With our son smiling at us from my mom's lap, and Simon and I in front of our loved ones, pledging to remain together until death do us part...

Today is definitely the best day of my life.

Also by Ava Nichols

Thank you for reading, **Bossy Grump Next Door**. If you loved this book, then you will love **The Billionaire Firefighter**!

It's a steamy and heart-warming story about being in love with the man of your dreams and having your deepest desires come true. It's a full-length, Brother's Best Friend, Enemies to Lovers Romance that offers a happily ever after and a surprise ending guaranteed to leave you breathless.

Click here and get it now: *The Billionaire Firefighter* - A Brother's Best Friend, Enemies to Lovers Romance

Here's a sneak peak:
My plan was to get my art career off the ground, *not* sleep with my brother's best friend... again...
Growing up, James Calder was always the hot, tall and dark, bad boy.
So, it was no surprise when he left town after our one hot, steamy night without saying goodbye. Not even to my brother.
Now, James is back as the newest firefighter in town. And this time, he's got secrets - his son being one of them.

Seeing his face again made my body tremble with anger, but also desire.

His charm always pulls me right back in. We're like two magnets that can't stay apart.

Next thing I know, things are firing up and cooking between us in my coffee shop.

And again, when we're stuck together at a winter lodge in a snowstorm.

He definitely knows how to heat and melt my body from head to toe.

I know I'm risking heartache again. And my brother will be upset if he finds out.

I thought this was already a recipe for disaster and then I found another ingredient – **I'm pregnant.**

Click here and get it now: *The Billionaire Firefighter* - A Brother's Best Friend, Enemies to Lovers Romance

The Billionaire Firefighter
Sneak Peak

My plan was to get my art career off the ground, *not* sleep with my brother's best friend... again...

Growing up, James Calder was always the hot, tall and dark, bad boy.

So, it was no surprise when he left town after our one hot, steamy night without saying goodbye. Not even to my brother.

Now, James is back as the newest firefighter in town. And this time, he's got secrets - his son being one of them.

Seeing his face again made my body tremble with anger, but also desire.

His charm always pulls me right back in. We're like two magnets that can't stay apart.

Next thing I know, things are firing up and cooking between us in my coffee shop.

And again, when we're stuck together at a winter lodge in a snowstorm.

He definitely knows how to heat and melt my body from head to toe.

I know I'm risking heartache again. And my brother will be upset if he finds out.

I thought this was already a recipe for disaster and then I found another ingredient — **I'm pregnant.**

Click here and get it now: *The Billionaire Firefighter* - A Brother's Best Friend, Enemies to Lovers Romance

Chapter One - Tessa

I'm wiping down the counters of the shop when the bell jingles over the front door. "We're closed!"

I really need to remember to lock that door, I remind myself, only for my thoughts to be interrupted. "It's me!"

"Hey!" I look up and grin at my sister-in-law. Well, almost sister-in-law. Sara's marrying my brother, Ben. They're disgustingly, ridiculously happy; it makes my heart hurt to look at them sometimes.

Sara's dark red-brown curls bounce as she rushes up to me and slaps her hands on the counter. "You are never gonna believe what I just found out."

"They're doing the annual ski race in clown costumes," I say, deadpan.

"Ha, ha, ha. Although actually, I'd watch the race if they did that."

Despite the fact that we live in a tourist town that gets most of its business from the ski tourists every winter, Sara is not what you'd call an outdoors-y kind of girl. I am, I love nature, and a lot of my artwork is inspired by the woods around me. I grew up here, and I know this place is in my bones because of how it shows up in my art all the time.

"No." Sara's wiggling with excitement, her brown eyes sparkling. "Guess who's back in town. Go on, guess!"

"Uh, I don't know, a celebrity?" We've had a few who come through town for the skiing.

"Oh my God, you're no fun." Sara grins. "It's *James Calder.*"

It's a good thing I'm wiping down the counters and not

holding a coffee cup, because I would've dropped it as my fingers go slack and my jaw pops open.

"I. Know. Right?" Sara has no idea that she's giving me a heart attack for all the wrong reasons. "Ben is so excited! He just got off the phone with him. James flies in tomorrow! Ben's going to pick him up from the airport."

"Oh?" I manage faintly.

I need to get it together. I need to act excited and casual about this. James is my older brother's best friend. They were inseparable growing up. And Sara can never, ever know the real reason that James left, because Ben can never know the reason why James left.

They can't find out it's all my fault.

"He didn't say why he's coming back," Sara continues, oblivious to my distress. "Or why he left. Ben didn't want to pry but of course he's curious."

"Mm." I quickly begin wiping everything up again. I need to finish closing up the coffee shop anyway, and it'll keep me occupied so that I don't have to show Sara my face. I'm a painter, not an actress, for a reason, mainly because I'm a terrible liar.

"Oh, are you all alone?" Sara asks.

"Yeah, Jenny has an exam."

Our town balloons in size during the tourist season but the year-round residents are a lot fewer, so most of the people who work for me in my coffee shop are the local high school students. It's usually a win-win since Sara and I can handle things the rest of the year during school hours by ourselves, and when we're busy, the kids out of school anyway, and the kids get good work experience and some money for college.

But sometimes, like right now when there's an exam coming up, it means I close up the coffee shop on my own.

"Here, let me help." Sara jumps behind the counter.

Thankfully, she's focused on getting us both out of here, so she stops talking about James. But my heart continues to hammer in my throat.

Will James tell Ben the truth? No, he wouldn't do that. James knows that Ben would kill the both of us for it.

I can't even imagine the pain on my brother's face if he knew that I slept with his best friend.

My crush on James throughout our years together had been going on for so long it felt like a part of me, and it had never occurred to me that James might ever like me back. I was just the kid sister tagging along.

But then I'd gone off to college, and when I'd come back for breaks... I could feel the tension. I'd tried hard to fight it, even as my heart had raced every time James was near me. The heat in his eyes as he looked at me had driven me insane.

James was the bad boy of our town. I was constantly hearing about his exploits with my brother while we were growing up, as they ran around town causing havoc. Ben was generally the one pulling James out of scrapes, which I knew made him more attractive to some of the girls around town, but in my opinion, even if Ben hadn't been my brother... yeah, I had a thing for a boy with a bit of an edge to him.

It didn't hurt that James was insanely handsome. He'd had a brief gangly awkward phase, but by the time I went to college, he had filled out, built up, sporting a strong jawline and a constant hint of stubble. His hair had gotten darker as he'd gotten older until it was a dark brown that was almost black, but his eyes remained the same intense blue that they always had been.

On the day of my graduation, it had all come to a head.

Ben hadn't wanted to deal with my graduation party, and I understood why. Nobody wants to be the escort for their little sibling while that sibling's partying with all their friends. But my parents had wanted someone to check on me, so Ben had sent James.

I can still hear the music in my head when I remember dancing, throwing my body into it, and feeling James watching me with a searing look. I can feel the phantom of his hands on my hips when the tension snapped and he pressed up against me from behind, his touch searing into me.

He'd danced with me, his body grinding against mine, and I'd felt him growing hard against my ass. I'd let him take more and more of my weight until my head was against his shoulder and his hand was dangerously close to sliding down my pants.

The air around us had felt charged with electricity as years of desire had come crashing down around us. I didn't know how long James had wanted me. I still don't know now, since I never got the courage to ask him. I didn't want to be the idiot who confessed she'd had such a long-standing crush only to find out it wasn't reciprocated, and given what happened afterwards, I think I was right in my choice.

But at the time, I'd been filled with a daring that I seemed to have everywhere in my life except for romance, and I'd leaned in and kissed his neck.

James had groaned, a sound I hadn't been able to hear over the music, but I had felt against my lips, and he'd grabbed my chin to tilt my head up and kiss me.

And what a kiss it was.

If I'm being honest with myself, it was the best kiss of

my life. I've tried to get things started with a few of the tourists who roll in every year but none of them give me the spark that James did. I know it's probably ridiculous of me to keep thinking about it, but if nobody can beat him, then what's the point? I know what my standards are now.

And God was it a good kiss.

James kissed me slick and deep like the world was ending. I'd melted against him. I would've done anything he wanted in that moment, so long as he kept kissing me. We kept swaying to the music, just barely technically dancing, his mouth devouring down my throat as I panted up at the ceiling.

He'd touched me with such confidence, nothing like the college boys I'd tried to have something with. Those had been rushed and clumsy and I'd always felt a bit like they didn't really know what they were doing, but they never asked me anything—never asked me what I liked, or what they should do. They just went for it and made me feel like raw steak and they were dogs slobbering over me.

James was different. He touched me like he knew my body already, with a confidence and skill that had me breathless.

It was a college party, everyone buzzed around us with the high of both alcohol and being a graduate, so nobody had paid us any attention. It had still felt like the most delicious kind of debauchery when James had stuck one hand down my pants and another up my shirt, toying with my breast and rubbing his fingers over my lace panties.

"Please," I'd begged. I hadn't been able to get any other words out. *"Please...."*

I'd thought he might make me orgasm right there on the dance floor, but he'd wrenched his hands away and pulled me through the crowd until we'd found the laundry room.

Any shame I might've had, technically having sex in some fraternity's house, was nonexistent. I had wanted him too badly.

He'd picked me up and set me on top of the washer like I weighed nothing, and I'd been able to feel his arms flexing under my hands, making me shiver. My legs had spread automatically and he'd rocked against me, showing me exactly how much he wanted me.

As I remember it now, I'm embarrassed. I was so obviously desperate, whining and begging for him, blabbering a bunch of stupid things about how long I'd wanted this, how hot he was, how good he felt.

But my embarrassment now is a few years too late. At the time, I hadn't cared. He'd been everything I wanted, and I was helpless to stop myself from begging for him.

We'd practically torn at each other's clothes until he was sliding into me, and I'd had to bite down on his shoulder to try and muffle the noises I was making. I hadn't had much to drink and neither had he, but I felt completely intoxicated on him, the feeling of him thrusting into me, how full I felt, the way that he growled in my ear and kissed me like we were dying.

I wrapped my legs around him and felt just how strong and tall he was compared to me, how much power he had in his body as he fucked me just the right amount of rough. I felt like a naughty girl for the first time in my life but in the best way possible.

The way he'd kissed me all over, yanking my top up so he could mouth at my breasts and suck at my nipples, made me feel like I was being devoured. Like just maybe he actually wanted me as desperately as I wanted him.

He'd had his hand around my neck, his thumb pressing under my jaw to tilt my head up, so that I had no way to muffle my moans as I'd orgasmed around him. It had felt so fucking *good*, and he hadn't stopped, thrusting into me, chasing his own high and drawing out my own so that I was shivering with sensitivity by the time I felt him come inside me.

We'd made out frantically, still wrapped around each other, until someone had banged on the door and we'd separated with wild laughter.

I'd passed out in the car on the way home, exhausted, and he and Ben had smuggled me back into the house so our parents wouldn't know how late I'd stayed out.

When I woke up the next morning, I'd been groggy, and slightly hungover, but full of joy and hope. I had worried about Ben, of course, but that concern had been overridden with my excitement over James... until I got the news.

James had left in the middle of the night, and hadn't come back to town since.

Until now.

"Are you okay?"

"Ow!" I jerk my head up and bang it on the underside of the counter.

I've been on my knees staring at the bags of coffee for who knows how long and Sara's looking at me with concern. "Did you hear anything I just said?"

No, no I didn't. I was a little busy remembering the best sex of my life. "I'm sorry, no, I didn't."

Sara grins. "It's okay. I know it was a long day. I was just saying, I forgot to tell you the juiciest part of the whole thing with James."

"Oh, do tell." I'm shocked I can make my voice sound salacious instead of pained. I don't want to hear any gossip about the man who broke my heart and skipped town on both me and my brother.

Sara leans in, grinning. "He's got a *son*."

It's even worse than I feared.

Click here and get it now: *The Billionaire Firefighter* - A Brother's Best Friend, Enemies to Lovers Romance

About the Author

Ava Nichols writes relatable, sexy, and heartfelt contemporary romance. Her stories have a balance of fun, edginess, steam, light-heartedness and depth. You'll get to watch her characters grow, open up their hearts and eventually find a happily ever after.

Her favorite themes are Billionaire Bad Boys, Enemies to Lovers, Brother's Best Friend, Boss, Second Chance, and Age Gap.

When she's not reading or writing, she's enjoying nature, dance, pilates and spending time with her family. She lives in Southern California with her husband, two young children and two small dogs.

Join Ava's newsletter to receive a FREE copy of her book, *My Billionaire SEAL Protector*, plus news on upcoming releases, giveaways, free reads and more! https://BookHip.com/RSKPXRM

Printed in Great Britain
by Amazon

38212547R00138